Brothers

D1270295

Paul Mohrbacher

keen editions

ISBN: 978-0-9846603-5-3

Book design by Ryan Scheife / Mayfly Design
Cover artwork composed from images: (image # 158539862) © Pushish Donhongsa/iStockphoto; (image # 141411661) © icsnaps/iStockphoto; (image #92102933) © Ryan Jorgensen/iStockphoto.
Author photograph courtesy of Andrea Cole Photography

Published by Keen Editions and printed in Canada.

For my grandchildren

If your brother wrongs you, remember not so much his wrongdoing
but more than ever that he is your brother,
that he was brought up with you.

— EPICTETUS, ENCHIRIDION, 43

As a kid growing up in Bismarck, North Dakota, I'd walked by hundreds of street people. I always looked straight through them, or crossed the street to avoid them. My brother used to cross the street to avoid them, too. Until he became one. And then he became a ward of the state, the state of California. It felt like a marginal difference to me.

I'd flown half way across the country to see him, so avoiding him wasn't an option. There he stood: wearing a clean shirt that was way too warm for this end-of-August weather. A cigarette hung from his mouth and protruded from a gap between his two front teeth. His hands shook, not like Parkinson's, more like agitation or anger. I was shaking, too.

His caretakers probably saw my visit differently, but I had one reason for being in San Mateo, and only one: to have a conversation with him about the most painful chapter in my life. Would he punch me? Would I punch him? Both distinct possibilities.

He smiled and blinked with eyes I recognized: the eyes of a guy who'd had places to go, not enough sleep and too many drugs too many times.

"Where you been, brother?" he said, in an accusing tone. He was never a big man, maybe five feet seven inches, but he had gone soft, his belly pushing out from under the shirt. He was sixty-five, but looked more like seventy-five. I was three years younger. We hadn't seen each other for twelve years—or spoken for six.

I was slow to step away from the van. I finally knocked some words together. "Same as always. Bismarck, North Dakota." I approached him.

"The brother who never left home, right? Bloomed where

he was planted, right? Hey, bro, welcome to the state of altered consciousness!" He opened his arms wide. We hugged. He might have looked ragged, but his embrace still had plenty of oomph.

My hug was ambiguous, tentative. Did he feel me pull back? I could tell from his wet hair that he had just showered, but he still smelled of cigarettes and perspiration. But he was straight. No alcohol, no drugs at the Sunnyslope Board and Care Home. The cigarette slipped from his mouth onto the sidewalk. He looked at it helplessly.

When we drew apart, he said, "Retrieve my Marlboro, will you, brother?"

I picked it up and handed it to him. It went right back into the gap and fluttered as he talked. "Thanks, and welcome to San Mateo, brother. It doesn't get any better than this." He swept his arm around as if taking in an estate instead of a cheaply built group home.

Oh, I knew things could get a lot better than this. The same old Nick was coming out, the guy who if he were sinking into a pile of manure would remark, "It doesn't get any better than this, as shit goes." It wasn't that he was sanguine about life. It was that he couldn't see what a mess he had made of his own life, much less of mine.

I forced myself to look him in the eye. "Hey, Nick, I'm glad to see you." It didn't even sound convincing to me.

He only had eyes for the van. "Nice wheels. Let's go." He shuffled toward the rental van I had picked up at the San Francisco airport. He was ready to be sprung.

A year ago, I'd had a phone call from a San Francisco hospital. Nick had been found unconscious in Golden Gate Park. My conscience had yelped: "You're his brother, for Christ's sake. How can you *not* go to San Francisco?" But I didn't. A couple of months after the hospital call, I got a message from the people who ran Sunnyslope, my brother's new home in the Bay area. They begged me to visit him. They knew he had a sibling back in North Dakota—a brother who had apparently dropped Nick from his life. So here I was, months later, at Sunnyslope, a few miles up a hill from downtown San Mateo

I had arrived on a late flight the evening before and went to a bed and breakfast near downtown San Mateo. I lingered over breakfast at the lovely old house on Palm Avenue while I read *The New York Times* and half-watched the televised coverage of Princess Diana's death. My daughters, Clare and Frances, both married and living on the East Coast, had called me early that morning to tell me about Diana's accident. They were heartbroken, as if she were a relative. They wanted me to call them after I'd seen Nick. They didn't say it right out, but they weren't happy I'd kept him out of their lives all these years.

The plan was for me to take Nick out for the day. José, one of the staff, said Nick would be ready to go right after I met the staff. They were eager to see me, he assured me. That was just what I feared. They would lecture me about my duty to Nick. They would play on my guilt—*he needs you*. But they had it wrong. I needed something from him.

I was here for three days, but it couldn't pass quickly enough for me. Teacher prep week at Bismarck High School started next week. I'd told the principal I'd be back in time.

"José said I should come inside before we leave. And I want to see where you live." I looked at the one-story rambler, nailed to a flat, ground-level foundation. Anything in California looked flimsy to a North Dakotan, bred on the brick, stone, stucco and wood of homes built on level ground on flat prairie over a full basement.

I never could understand building a house on a steeply rising or falling hill. Houses here looked ready to slide down the incline into a deep, yawning fissure, one of a million sucking mouths of a sleeping fault. The sea was twenty miles away, but the fault was right beneath us, for all I knew, and this house looked ready to slide all twenty miles.

Nick's face froze in anger. "José said what? José doesn't know his ass...." At that moment, José opened the front door and smiled at us.

"Your brother's a real character, man," José said with a big smile. José was a stocky fellow in his thirties. He extended his hand. "Come on in. My sister will tell you about his insulin." So Nick was diabetic. Nick muttered something. José punched him playfully on the shoulder. "Hey, Nick, we still *amigos, si?*"

"Don't push your luck," Nick groused.

On the skinny front porch, two metal patio chairs flanked an enormous cigarette urn bursting with butts. We followed José into the living room, crowded with worn easy chairs grouped more or less in a circle around a cheap television resting on a TV cart. On the wall behind the cart was a framed image of the Virgin of Guadalupe.

A woman stood behind one of the chairs. "This is my sister Consuela," José said. "Hey, *sorella*, this is Nick's brother." Consuela looked like she was in her forties. Thin and diminutive, she kept pursing her lips. I assumed her reproachful demeanor was meant for me.

"Nice to meet you, Nick's brother."

I winced. That was to be my identity—Nick's brother. "Hi, Consuela. My name is Ben."

"His name is Ben." José echoed me. His eyes snapped back and forth between the two of us.

"Hi, Ben." She eyed me coldly. I could read her eyes—where have *you* been?

A shrill voice came from behind a door that started to swing out, revealing a kitchen stove. José said, "That's our sister, Frieda. She helps with the housework and does the cooking." José's role seemed to be "the *guy*," necessary for the all-female crew who ran a residence for heavily medicated men.

Frieda appeared from behind the door, wiping her hands on an apron. She was as thick as Consuela was thin. I nodded to her. She smiled.

"*Sorella*, this is Ben, Nick's brother.

"Are you hungry?" Frieda asked me. "Nick loves to eat."

"No thanks, Frieda. We're going out to dinner." She frowned a little. I tried an appeasing grin with no luck.

"You want to see Nick's room?" Consuela led me toward Nick's bedroom without waiting for an answer.

"How many men live here?" I asked.

"Four," she said as she opened the bedroom door. Nick and Barney were in one bedroom, two others in a second. Nick had stayed back in the living room to "keep an eye on the van."

The bedroom had a hospital ward feel, three beds lined up against a wall with rollout windows looking out on a small patch of grass. One bed was neatly made, its bedside table empty. So Sunnyslope was below capacity. A recent death? On the middle bed, a man looking to be in his sixties lay on top of the spread, clothed except for his shoes. "That's Barnabas," Consuela said. "He goes by 'Barney.' Hey, Barney. Nick's brother, Ben." Consuela wasted no words.

"Hi, Barney," I said and waved a little hello. He barely waved a finger back. He seemed to be in a trance, listening to some scratchy country music on a little alarm-clock radio perched on the bed stand.

"Barney is one helluva guy," Nick yelled from the living room. Barney did not register the compliment.

Nick's wrinkled bedspread featured an image of the Golden Gate Bridge. On his dresser a radio and a pack of cigarettes shared space with a matchbook and a plastic water glass. No pictures, no snapshots of a life.

Consuela and I returned to the living room. Nick was pacing, looking anxious to go. "Barney is the model for why this place is called Sunnyslope—right, José? 'Sunnyslope,' as in 'Enjoy the ride downhill, old fart.'" I didn't smile. The joke was at Barney's expense.

José turned on the TV, ignoring Nick. I felt claustrophobic and was suddenly grateful that Nick wanted to escape in the van.

I looked at Consuela. "How's he getting along?" She smiled stiffly.

"Like a prince!" Nick shouted. "I am the goddamn prince of get-along, I am the-one-who-plays-well-with-others." His voice held an old hint of anger, a tone familiar to me. Nick had always had a quick temper growing up. Quick to accuse me of not doing my assigned chores at home, quick to take offense over being called on the carpet by our parents for his obvious screw-ups with his chores. Had he mellowed? Nick liked these people, I thought. They liked him. He just couldn't stop talking over them. Nothing new there.

Consuela wagged a finger at Nick. "Your brother likes to swear and shock us," she sighed. José giggled. Nick listened to her and inserted another Marlboro into his mouth, leaving it unlit.

"He's okay," she offered. "He lets us give him his insulin shots. He keeps his bed and his dresser clean. He eats good. He only smokes outside. But he smokes too much."

Nick nodded. He clearly respected Consuela. He patted his stomach. "The food is first-class, Frieda's cooking is legendary on the peninsula. Three-star."

Frieda smiled.

Consuela smiled too. Was she feeling nervier? "He talks about you a lot. I'm glad you came." She avoided my gaze.

He'd come to Sunnyslope ten months ago and I was pretty sure I was his first guest. I didn't blame them for wondering how a brother could ignore a sibling in as precarious a state as Nick's.

"You stay for a week maybe." Consuela didn't ask. She strongly recommended.

"Only three days, Consuela. I teach high school back in North Dakota. Classes start pretty soon." I wanted to change the subject, to make her feel good. "So, you're doing wonders with him. Nick seems like a pretty good lodger." That was a safe guess. He was never one to lie around. He loved throwing parties, and when alone, he could entertain himself. He was smart, funny and comfortable around strangers, even if he made others uncomfortable with his know-it-all attitude. And, my god, he was sober now.

"He's pretty good," Consuela said. "And the people at Elder Town say he is lots of fun."

"Elder Town, that's the day program here in San Mateo," José explained.

Nick shook his pelvis. "Where seniors get down!" Consuela blushed. José giggled and switched channels to a Univision soap opera.

Still standing in the kitchen doorway, Frieda clucked and wagged a finger at Nick. He blew her a kiss. "Frieda and I are going to elope and run away to Baja California, where we will open a little taco shop—Nick and Frieda's Taqueria. Don't forget, Frieda. You promised me." Frieda brushed him off with a wave of her chubby hand and disappeared into the kitchen.

"Nick, go to your room and change into a nice shirt and pants. You can't go to the ballet looking like that."

"Yes, Consuela." Nick submitted docilely. I had never seen Nick deferential. Ever. Consuela had Nick under control. There were a few more minutes of awkward silence in the living room while Nick changed in his bedroom.

"Bismarck is nice?" Consuela asked over the din.

"Yes, very nice," I said. "Nice and warm during the summer. Gets a little cold in winter, though. And we had a bad flood back there in April. Pretty much destroyed the downtown in Grand Forks." Had she ever heard of Grand Forks?

"Maybe you stay in California?" she said. "Closer to Nick."

"Well," I paused, "we'll see."

"You come live here then."

Nick returned in an open-collar shirt, an old-fashioned cardigan and wrinkled chinos. I wore the same, only mine fit better.

"Your fly's open," I said.

He jerked the zipper up and muttered, "The captain's privilege."

"He's had his insulin shot," Consuela said. "Watch what he eats. And no alcohol." Nick shot her a mean look. She glared right back. "If he has alcohol, he can get very sick. Sometimes he wets his pants. He's wearing senior diapers."

My brilliant brother, Nick, PhD, was wearing senior diapers.

"Purely precautionary," Nick said.

"There's an extra pair in his pack," she said. José had slipped the strap of a small kit over Nick's shoulder. "There's orange juice in there too."

"Also some super size Trojans and a little address book," Nick added.

I tried hard not to roll my eyes.

José turned off the TV and stood to escort Nick out to the van. I followed them to the door, and then turned to Consuela, who had ignored the Trojan comment. "I'm happy to meet you, Consuela. Sunnyslope seems like just what Nick needs."

Ignoring the compliment, she said, "You come back a lot, now. Nick likes company."

"It's been a long time, I know." I promised I'd get him back early tonight.

He cut me off. "We're going to take San Fran captive today and tonight, Señora," Nick announced. "The ballet, dinner, damsels—who knows? Don't expect us before four tomorrow morning." He pushed open the door and made for the lawn while I shook Consuela's hands and waved to Frieda.

"Is midnight okay?" I asked. Consuela nodded gravely.

Out on the porch, the chairs were now occupied by the two other lodgers, smoking.

"These two captains of industry are Arnie and Rudy," Nick announced. "Arnie's the short one and Rudy's the fat one."

I said hello to Arnie and Rudy. Like Nick, both of them wore hand-me-downs, shirts too short or pants too long, scuffed, and untied running shoes. Neither had shaved for days, and on their scalps strands of hair stood clumped together in the odd patches left by sleep. They waved and kept on smoking. They were several shades more comatose than Barney. But they could sure suck in those cigarettes. Arnie puckered when he inhaled and then blew smoke out in a long, curling arc.

José, Nick and I approached the van. Nick went around to the passenger side and started to get in. First he sat on the seat with both feet dangling. Then he swung one leg onto the floor. He sat facing out the side, breathing hard, one leg out in the street, one on the floorboard. Should I help him? He looked as helpless as a flipped-over turtle. Finally, with his right arm he pulled the right leg inside and slammed the door shut with more energy than I thought he had in him.

"Let's get this motherfucker off the ground," he panted.

José smiled. "Bye, Nick. Be good."

"I define what's good, my man," Nick responded as he tossed the small kit with his medications into the back seat. I waved at José and backed the van into a neighbor's driveway. A woman came out of the house and waved to Nick. He blew her a kiss. We drove down the hill toward downtown San Mateo on our way to the ballet in San Francisco.

"You drive, I'll sleep." Nick smiled as he said it. "Miles to go."

His drive-sleep line brought me back. When I was around eight and Nick was eleven, we played cops and robbers at bedtime. Our bedposts acted as our joysticks as we hurtled off down the imaginary highway, one driving, the other sleeping but really keeping an eye open for gun-toting roadies. Our beds were always heading west, toward San Francisco. Our dad was fond of saying, "Here in flat, old North Dakota, on a clear night you can look out the window and see San Francisco." We believed him, even if it was only Mandan we saw.

Nick had touched a common thread of shared childhood. Long-term memory was working. Alone out here, two thousand miles west of North Dakota and a million miles away mentally, my brother had hung on to at least one thin strand of family ties. I'd cut all of them between us. "Miles to go" was right.

A gorgeous Sunday afternoon in San Francisco, blue skies, breezy, in the seventies. A free outdoor performance in Stern

Grove. A parking spot close by. A lot to like.

"Free entertainment for the masses!" Nick shouted to a stranger after we found a parking spot six blocks from Stern Grove. It was right next to the bus stop. "We scored, bro!" And a lot to fear.

A bus materialized. It was jammed. Nick needed help navigating the bus steps. I pushed and steadied and pushed some more until he was inside. I paid the fares. We stood for the six blocks.

"Here comes Sloat Boulevard and the Stern Grove Festival," the bus driver announced. "This Bay Area tradition on summer Sundays has lasted almost six decades. Grab your picnic basket and enjoy the free music down there. Today's your last chance: this is the last show of 1997."

Nick clapped. "Thank you, my man," he shouted, loud enough for the entire bus to hear. "This is my brother from Bismarck, North Dakota. Enn-Dee for short."

"Welcome the brother from Bismarck to San Francisco!" the driver droned into the intercom. I turned and waved. Nobody from the coast would know Bismarck from Timbuktu. There was a little clapping as riders queued up at the doors. "Enjoy your stay!" someone said as the bus emptied out.

We walked over to a shuttle bus and climbed aboard for the descent down to the esplanade of Stern Grove. I gawked like a Midwesterner as the world above the slope disappeared. Giant eucalyptus, redwood and fir trees stood thick along the steep downhill road. Within minutes we were on the floor of the ravine. I overheard someone tell a friend that the grove was about sixty feet below street level.

We stepped off the shuttle bus and followed the crowd across the esplanade to the Concert Meadow, a flat, bowl-shaped expanse, the "grove" of Stern Grove. People were dining at small white tables or sitting on camp chairs in front of a huge stage facing the natural amphitheater. Above us, thousands of people spread out on the hillsides. They were lying on blankets, sitting on campstools, perching on tree limbs. Their scattered blankets created a patchwork quilt effect. The higher and wider I looked, the more I saw people who were barely able to see the stage through the leaves and branches. They were there to listen, even if they couldn't see.

Amazing. My mood brightened. We could enjoy outdoor ballet together in a spectacular setting. I was glad I had read about this place in a travel article: "Stern Grove: San Fran's Hidden Treasure."

We needed a place to sit. We'd arrived later than the picnickers. We showed up without blankets or folding chairs or visor caps. I knew we looked unprepared, not dressed quite right. No way was Nick fit for climbing up among the blankets, campstools and ice chests. And the grass was still damp and slippery in spots.

"Lady Luck, find us a place to park our sorry asses," Nick growled. I grunted agreement. We scoured the bottom of the hill for some vacant grass. Nothing. Then, like the Red Sea parting, a patch of green appeared. An obliging clutch of young people shifted their blankets to make room for us.

I thanked them, all fresh-faced college-age kids. And the grass here was only slightly damp from yesterday's fog. We tossed a couple of glossy ballet programs onto the ground. I helped Nick lower himself onto his program and sat down on mine. Our butts spilled around them and I could feel the dampness spread.

Soon our tanned young neighbors on the blanket were passing us fruit and pretzels and water. "Capital!" Nick shouted. "Thanks for sharing!" Crunching pretzels, he leaned over as the orchestra tuned. "Scoring is everything, bro."

He loved sex-tinged imagery in describing everyday life. We'd scored because we found a place to park. And a place to sit. We'd scored because he was living at Land's End and not in North Dakota. And because it was a beautiful day, full of promise.

He leaned over to me, like he was reading my mind. "Life is not all sex, as much as I would wish it so. The life of culture counts high. I pray to Terpsichore, goddess of dance, every day. And she descends upon us here, today, in Stern Grove. But Aphrodite, goddess of love, lurks nearby. Watch me pick up two lovelies to accompany us the rest of the day and evening, and possibly through the night. Did you notice the pair behind us?" I hadn't noticed them. I didn't turn. Nick, the senior stud, on the prowl, eager to score.

The San Francisco Ballet performed several modern dance pieces, and then selections from *Coppelia*. These kids could dance! Their talent was backed by ensemble precision and youthful energy. Nick directed the entire performance with little hand motions in front of his chest. Music had been one of my bonds with him. He was the one who introduced me to classical music, who lectured me on the finer points of jazz. A long time ago. I'd almost forgotten. I'd forgotten a lot about him and me. Forgetting made it easier for me.

He had initiated me into just about every facet of young life. As the older brother, he was my guide from puberty through adolescence to young adulthood. He was the gregarious kid who knew more than I did. More about life, about people, about nearly everything.

Our parents both worked long hours. He and I were together a lot. He mentored me about sex and girls, about staying out late, about the kids I should be hanging out with. I didn't always follow his lead. My cautious personality led me down different paths.

He was taking music lessons and knew how to read music by seventh grade. He started playing the bass fiddle at fifteen. He started attending orchestra performances at sixteen. I avoided learning an instrument and seldom attended concerts. My academic interests lay in sports and ancient languages, Greek and Latin. We were both quirky North Dakota kids, but in different ways.

In high school, he surrounded himself with girls. He was friends with many, intimate with some. I had a grand total of two girlfriends in four years of high school, and I never moved beyond necking in the back seat. He, a declared non-virgin at sixteen, never married. I married at twenty-five, a virgin until my wedding night.

He had a series of girlfriends, but he could never commit to any of them. I married Jeanne Marie, my high school sweetheart. A veteran of two marriages, he never had kids. Jeanne Marie and I had two daughters, two years apart.

He left Bismarck to gather graduate degrees in clinical psychology, while I was an undergraduate concentrating on the Greek and Roman classics at a local Catholic college. When he was home on vacation, we'd spend hours arguing about the incest between Oedipus the king and his mother, Jocasta — culpable or inculpable? Or about the Greeks' fascination with the irrational even as they laid philosophical foundations for Western thought. We fought over the great Stoic philosophers, Zeno, Epictetus and Marcus Aurelius. I believed the people of North Dakota were stoics because of winter's brutal harshness and the prairie's unrelenting vastness. I thought we were resilient, too. Nick saw us as culturally deprived, noble but narrow.

I started teaching Latin at Bismarck High School, where many students took four years of it — Caesar, Cicero, Virgil, Horace, Ovid. I stayed on the prairie, and kept on teaching them year after year. Nick moved around. After a job at a counseling center in the Twin Cities, he worked in Chicago, Saint Louis, Denver and Seattle. Then, in San Francisco, he went to work for the V.A. Hospital.

He was the fox, racing through fields of study in quick succession, tracking the shifting pathways of the brain. I was the hedgehog, burrowing into my field. My grand scheme was to link Athens and Rome with Bismarck, helping students see the relevance of Latin and classical learning in deciphering the blur of messages their culture was feeding them every day.

His career as a clinical psychologist sounded interesting and hip, and mine sounded predictable and square. The same for our dress codes. He dressed in colorful plaid jackets and madras pants with buckled loafers. He slummed in a poncho and jeans. My students called me Mister Rogers.

Now here we were together, sharing music. The sun pierced Stern Grove in bright shafts of light. The eucalyptus scent was dizzying. The dancers swirled, the audience swayed, and Léo Delibes' music echoed off the hillside—all under fir trees whose branches seemed to wave in tempo.

I looked at Nick, who was kind of gyrating in place. A show for the two women behind us? He turned and whispered in my ear. "I want you to know, bro, that I am Nick Dancer, the star dancer at Elder Town."

"What?"

"The day activity center."

I nodded and looked away. I wanted him to stop talking.

"There are seniors so shy they never get off their asses. First I serenade them. Then I bring them into the circle. I guide them to the floor, oozing charm." His voice was getting louder.

"Okay. Tell me later."

"You should see me. I convince them they are royalty. They dance. I expose their inner beauties!

Suddenly, he nearly shouted. "Look at that!"

"That" was a series of grand jumps by a muscular member of the ballet corps. It epitomized abandon. In rapt response, two thousand hillside occupants whistled and cheered and clapped.

"*Muy especiale!*" he shouted in what I was sure was the only Spanish he knew. "*Muy especiale!*" he repeated.

Onstage there was a pause for a scene change. With no warning, somebody sitting above me on the hillside slid straight down into my back. The impact was not concussive. It was soft, almost an embrace. I guessed the slider was one of the women Nick was doing reconnaissance on. I turned. Sure enough.

As she extricated herself from me she whispered, "I'm so

sorry! The grass is really slippery! Are you okay?" She stood and brushed her slacks off. Nick turned to examine the slider.

"A fallen woman!" he said with mock dignity. People around us giggled and smiled.

"I'm okay. No problem," I assured her, standing up. "Here, I'll help you back to your blanket." She looked embarrassed but smiled as she took my hand, turned and climbed back up.

She brushed herself off, and sat down. "Thank you. I'll dig in deeper!" The slider was African American. Her friend was white. They shared a blanket held firm by a poncho staked to the ground. Okay, I thought, let the games begin.

Despite the pause onstage, Nick continued wagging his conducting finger, as if to say, "Look, I've conjured up two lovelies." He turned to face the slider's companion.

"Your turn," he said. She blushed bright red.

As I sat down again on the program, he pushed an elbow into my side. He whispered something about singing leading to dancing, and dancing leading to revelry.

That was my brother, Nick Dancer. He connected with people through music, dancing, singing, playing his bass fiddle. He used to have a bass fiddle. He used to have a car. He used to have an apartment. He used to have a life. All gone. Now, just the remnants of a life.

Whenever Nick appeared in my dreams—more than I wanted—he was flying and giddily singing away. Often he would be flashing as well, pulling back an overcoat to reveal his privates. As a young man I felt he was unsure about his sexuality, but very sure about his soaring power over people, especially women. Over the years I had listened to endless stories of his sexual exploits, glossy tales of assignations there for the picking, the low-hanging fruit provided by Aphrodite. I didn't believe most of the stories, but they added up to a lot of scoring. And it intimidated me.

So what about our two new friends? A couple of fiftyish women out for a little fun? Back in North Dakota, I had never encountered this type of aggressive female, anybody who'd pull a stunt like this. Oh, I knew North Dakota was full of hard-nosed, brassy women on the make. But they'd get right in your face. These two were subtler, less obvious, more glamorous, less self-conscious.

And they must have sized us up as soon as we sat down. Both of us were older than they were, and we were not prize-winning males. Did they feel sorry for us? Or did we look interesting for other reasons?

The ballet continued to the final climactic scene. The corps members received three standing ovations. On the fourth, the slider tapped me on the shoulder. "We're wondering if you'd join us for a glass of wine at the bar?" I had my first real look at her. She wore her hair unbraided and had curly bangs. Flecks of gray peeked out here and there. Underneath all that hair was a great smile on a pixie face with a few wrinkles around the eyes. She wore jeans and a light blue sweater.

Her friend had short hair framing a pleasant round face that hinted at a kind of wistfulness. She was dressed in expensive-looking casual tan slacks and a silk jacket. No way was she going to muddy herself sliding into somebody.

Why us? Well, why not us? Most older men in this audience were with women who looked younger, or with male partners. Pickings were slim. Maybe the women had just decided, what the hell, these two are right here, let's have a drink with these harmless-looking characters.

"Always ready for a drink. Yes!" Nick volunteered.

She rolled her eyes. "My name is Joyce. And this is Bonnie," she laughed. Nick bowed to Bonnie.

"I'm Ben," I said flatly.

"And I am his brother, Doctor Nick," he said, with weird overtones of mystery and mastery.

"Ooh. What kind of doctor are you?" asked Joyce.

"I'm a psychologist."

"Oh. Not a real doctor."

Nick grimaced, lit a cigarette, sucked deeply on it and blew

16

smoke out the gap in his front teeth. "As the mind is more real than the body, it doesn't get more real than me." Bonnie nodded like she agreed with him.

We paired off, Joyce with me, Bonnie with Nick, and started walking toward the bar. Nick's gait was stiff, arthritic, but authoritative, like an old soldier.

Joyce kept up the patter. "You both live in the bay area?"

"Only me," Nick said. "Brother Ben is here for spiritual guidance."

"Bismarck, North Dakota," I said.

"San Francisco certainly specializes in alternative spiritual guidance," said Joyce. Nick overheard her.

"Ha," cried Nick. "You are a piece of work. Ben once was the rock star of ageless married love. Time wounds all heels, however, and he is an S.O.M., single older male. And I am his rock, his anchor, his better angel." We sat down at a table in the wine bar, and Nick shouted to the bartender, "I'll have a Sam Adams." I knew he didn't have a dime.

I wagged my head no to the bartender. "I may be the younger brother but I know my older brother is on several medications that will send him into convulsions and an early death if...."

Nick looked cross, mean, about to explode.

"...if he has any alcohol," I finished.

"Fuck that noise!" he shouted vehemently. Bonnie nudged Joyce.

"He and I'll have non-alcoholic beer," I said.

"The women will have Pinot Grigio, and this is on us. Reparation," said Joyce.

"My brother is the king of the caretakers, girls," Nick said. He cracked his knuckles and shot me a dirty look. "And a party pooper. Of course—he's a Latin teacher."

He had divulged my profession. That would drive them away, for sure. No fun to be had with someone so out of the mainstream, so un-hip.

"Really? How wonderful!" said Bonnie. Her first words.

"So Doctor Nick can help," Nick cajoled them. "What did you say your problems were?"

"We didn't," Joyce said. "So are you really brothers or is this an act?" Good, she sounded like a woman who'd been around the block.

Nick presented a wounded look. "We are most assuredly long lost brothers. I'm the prodigal. He's the favorite son. Our parents named him Ben. For Benedict. In Latin, the blessed one. They named me Nick. For ol' Nick, the devil."

"Why not for Saint Nicholas?" That was Bonnie, who seemed to be relishing this entire encounter, not a hint of jadedness in her bones. Maybe she'd never picked up a man before.

Nick shook his head and stroked his chin. "Doesn't fit my narrative. I prefer the devil motif. You know that prodigals end up wiser for their prodigal ways. I've lived here at Land's End forever. Brother here has just now arrived from the heartland to warm himself at the prodigal fire where I indeed have wasted my fortune in riotous living, so saith the Gospel."

As soon as the drinks came, he finished off his O'Doul's in one long, gurgling guzzle. Bonnie watched wide-eyed.

"Nick, what has the prodigal done to make himself a little devil?" Joyce ignored his beverage intake.

"He has broken all the family rules," Nick said, holding up all ten fingers. "We were two sons of North Dakota, keeping ourselves noble but narrow. I split and earned a PhD *cum laude* in clinical psychology, and headed West just in time to catch the big wave here in the 1970s, in old Baghdad by the Bay. Since then I've been putting people in touch with their intimate selves, restoring their wholeness. I chucked nobility for the real thing, I broke the bonds with mother and dad, dearly departed. And now here comes my brother to soak up ignobility and shake off the Midwest. Yazoo, brother!"

Would they figure out my brother was a ward of the county? Christ, they could see him now from the front: the half-ass shaving job, the lost teeth, the slight dribble of spittle when he spoke, the blotchy face, the balding head.

Not pretty, but, amazingly, not repulsive. He once was clearly the better looking of us. Okay, so neither of us was anybody's idea of a prize. We were about the same height. I was not as chubby as Nick, although I was developing a bit of girth. His hair was thinning, while I had a full gray mane. I looked a little younger than my age. But sixty-two is sixty-two. So what? I wasn't here to score. And Nick scoring? Only in his imagination. This was his day out, the first in many months. My goal was to exhaust him. I wanted to get him home without incident today so I could at least try to find out what I needed to know tomorrow. These two were incidents waiting to happen.

Joyce smiled. "How interesting. Bonnie just left the convent." Joyce sipped on her wine. Bonnie looked down at her glass and squirmed. Joyce went on. "After twenty-four years. I'm helping her build her confidence."

"Aha." Nick stroked his hairless chin. "Waiter, another fake one, please."

I nodded okay to the bartender. Nick leaned back in his chair. "Bonnie, welcome to the world. You came to the right place." Bonnie bit her lip. He smiled, a kind of professional, compassionate smile, no teeth showing, just a friendly upturn of the corners of his mouth. He had posed this way before, a thousand times. I was sure of it.

"I can help. Dancing may lead to wholeness." He took a healthy swig from the new bottle.

"Whatever that might mean," laughed Joyce.

"Are you or were you ever a Catholic?" Bonnie meant it to be funny, I thought.

Nick cleared his throat as if spitting something rotten out. "In No-Dak, our family was the fixed star of popery. Mother and dad sent us to the nuns through twelfth grade. I ejected from Rome early. Brother here hung on a few more decades, raising the kids Catholic and all that. I, being childless and humanistic, had no such commitment and certainly no propensity to carry on the faith."

"We're both what you'd call fallen-away Catholics," I said.

"But I think we have some idea of how difficult a decision this must have been for you. Right, Nick?" He nodded.

"Thank you. I'm doing fine, really," Bonnie said.

Nick turned to Joyce. "Every person contemplating life change needs an angel. Good for you, Angel Joyce. So Bonnie, what do you fear most: security, sexuality, or being dogged by a sense of wasted years?"

Like an exasperated athlete questioning a ref's call, Joyce interrupted: "Hey, there could be other options."

"I'm Doctor Nick. Didn't I say that?"

"You did, Nick," I said, and managed a wan smile at Joyce.

Bonnie grinned. She was game. "Okay. I fear mostly just catching up. I entered the convent at sixteen, and I'm forty-nine now and have a lot to learn. But...well, I have Joyce here, a master teacher."

Good, I thought, keep it light, don't even answer his question. Make this episode a simple rest stop on a breakout journey, not a deep encounter with my wild brother. Bonnie had the face of a younger woman—great freckles, a wide smile, thoughtful eyes and a trusting, naïve openness.

On the other hand, Joyce was svelte, her eyebrows plucked, her cheeks blushed and her lips touched with a pale lipstick. She exuded a woman-of-the-world aura, kind of weary. I liked that a lot.

"What did you do as a nun?" I asked Bonnie.

She fingered her glass. "I taught, I was a high school principal, and then I ran the education department for the Sacramento archdiocese. Sometimes Joyce makes it sound as though I slipped out of a time warp and arrived newborn on the world's doorstep."

Joyce looked at Bonnie. "You're my best friend and I worry about you, sweetheart. People—I mean divorced men—eat ex-nuns."

"I admit, it's a whole new world," replied Bonnie, "but I'm a quick study."

Joyce turned to us. "So—about the 'fallen woman' stunt—by the way, very funny, Nick—I checked you two out, okay? I whispered to Bonnie, 'Here, you want to meet a man without appearing outrageous?' I confess. You both looked harmless."

At that, Nick's eyes widened. I knew he wanted no part of harmless. She went on. "So I descended on you. Zoom, zoom!"

"Zoom, zoom yourself! *He* may be harmless" He pointed at me and snorted. "He'll vouch that I'm *not* harmless."

What was in his mind at that moment? That we were going back to some apartment with Bonnie and Joyce to enjoy a four-some roll in the hay? Had he forgotten where he lived? This was his first time in ten months out of a constrained environment. Maybe too much stimulation.

"And I checked that neither of you was wearing a ring. So we knew we weren't being home breakers," said Joyce.

I had just stopped wearing my wedding ring a month ago.

"I asked her to make sure before she slid," Bonnie added.

Nick made his move, seemingly emboldened by their precautions. "Younger brother and I are out for a day of it. Come with us to the Cliff House for supper. Let us entertain you." He played his pickup card. Joyce and Bonnie looked at each other.

"We have to be somewhere at seven," Joyce said. She was backing out. Nick was spooking her, I was sure. Good. He and I would do just fine alone.

"Sure, we would like that," said Bonnie. "We have time, Joyce." Bonnie's eyes were fixed on me. Was I endorsing Nick's gambit? Nick was right: I was the sensible one. Women liked that about me.

This *was* getting complicated. Three days here, that was my plan. I was here to reestablish contact with my brother, but their attention to us was kind of gratifying.

"Sounds okay," I said.

"Okay, meet you at the Cliff House at five." Joyce had also relented. "Let's go, Bonnie, it's a real hike up the hill. You two walking or riding?" She had to know Nick wasn't up to the half-mile climb out of the grove up to Sloat Boulevard.

"Riding, first class," Nick announced. Joyce left cash on

the table and the two women excused themselves. Bonnie looked excited, Joyce apprehensive. Chatting, laughing nervously, walking arm in arm, they turned and waved. The fog, cool and damp, was enveloping Stern Grove. As the women partly dissolved in the haze, Nick took my arm.

"Clearly, *Soeur* Bonnie has the hots for you, brother. But I think I can crack the cool shell of the Black sister without too much effort. Unless she's a follower of the lady from Lesbos. Notice we know nothing about her."

"Two hours doesn't leave much time for getting intimate." I was trying to cool him down.

"I am a master of the quick seduction."

"Nick, I don't want you messing around with them. I'm ready to kiss them both goodbye."

"Typical chickenshit North Dakotan. I promised you two lovelies."

"I never requested two lovelies," I countered.

"And I delivered them anyway. *Carpe diem*, brother." As if he had had anything to do with Joyce sliding down the hill.

I helped him out of his chair and we ambled over to the bus. We climbed aboard and found ourselves greeted by a chorus of senior citizens hunkered down in their seats and singing in uncertain unison, "I left my heart in San Francisco."

The driver shut the door and the bus started up the road. We joined in the singing. One minute we were picking up women, the next we were singing an old chestnut, eyes glued to a TV monitor scrolling the words and melody. Nick played the impresario, standing in the aisle, conducting with one arm while he hung on to a strap, and lustily proclaimed, "...because my love waits there." The bus had approached a knot of walkers, Bonnie and Joyce among them. He pointed at them. "I mean *there*." The two of them were busy talking, both at the same time, but Bonnie turned and waved to us. We waved back.

"Capital!" Nick barked. The bus riders applauded, and Nick blew them all a kiss.

That was the attractive side of Nick. He loved getting a

group of people involved in whatever he happened to be selling, whether it was self-help, the love of cars, the joy of sex, or the true path to happiness. Or just the pleasure of a sing-along. He was outrageous, but he somehow got by with it. Sly Nick was always engaged, even in his present damaged state. He was the extrovert. I was the introvert.

And then there was this side of him. "Well, you almost fucked that up, bro."

"What...?

"You were slow out of the gate for our friendly libation," Nick said triumphantly, "which is now to be followed by a friendlier liaison. I think Joyce has registered that the old boy is pretty foxy. Could you tell? She also had no ring—notice? She's got a story."

"Well, I haven't decided whether she is interested in you or me," I countered. "The Cliff House will tell." He scowled at me and smoothed his hair. I spent the rest of our ascent deciding whether to go back to San Mateo or on to the Cliff House.

Only when the shuttle bus emerged onto street level did I realize that there was still daylight left. After the shadowy netherworld of Stern Grove, the brightness of the fog-blurred late afternoon sun was shocking. We caught a city bus back to the car. I helped Nick onto the van seat. I'd decided we'd go to the Cliff House.

I drove up Nineteenth Avenue and headed west toward the ocean. "I bet they don't show," I jabbered.

Nick snorted. "Ho-ho, heave-ho; they *will* show, oh my bro. Or my name isn't Doctor Nick-o." He leaned forward like a hunting dog sniffing its quarry.

We pulled into the Cliff House parking lot twenty minutes later. They were already there. Nick pounded on the dash.

"Sonofabitch, what did Doctor Nick say? They showed. Pay up, brother."

They waved to us when we emerged from the van. I looked again. They really were attractive — Joyce in a sexy way, Bonnie in a vulnerable, open-to-the-world way. I was nervous. I had a sick man out on a day pass and we were picking up women. Or, were they picking us up?

"Hi," I shouted tentatively across the parking lot. "You must have had a police escort." Bonnie laughed and Joyce whispered something to her. As we joined up on the sidewalk, Nick was walking with difficulty, shuffling as if he were on an icy North Dakota sidewalk.

The iconic Cliff House stood on a rocky height above Ocean Beach and the Pacific Ocean. I had read about the views and asked the hostess for a table in the Bistro with a view of North Rock and its colony of seals. The seals seemed content just crawling over each other. In the first awkward seconds as we chose our chairs and looked down on the seals, I realized the writhing critters were grist for Nick's joke mill.

"I'll have what they're having," he announced.

It could have been a lot worse. "Apologies to Nora Ephron," I said. Joyce laughed hard, and Bonnie's face turned crimson. He was a very happy guy right now, entertaining the women. Even in his addled state, he had moxie.

Bonnie and Joyce stuck with white wine, and I ordered non-alcoholic beer for us.

Nick glared at me. "Excuse me, sisters. I'm off to the john," he huffed.

"No stopping at the bar."

"You are an imperious asshole," Nick said.

Joyce spit out a little of her wine.

"Thank you, I think," I said, and announced that I'd given the hostess ten dollars for the barman with the message there were to be no drinks for Nick.

"You are also an impecunious asshole," Nick said as he got up.

Bonnie and Joyce both laughed at his remark and stared at

him as he lurched away. Bonnie put her hand on my arm. "Tell us about your brother. Whatever you want to share."

Sure, why not tell them? And I needed to talk to somebody beside Consuela and José. Even six hours with Nick felt stressful.

I told them I'd gotten a call from a social worker in the Kaiser Permanente hospital system a year ago. Nick had been found in a diabetic coma in Golden Gate Park and was taken to San Francisco General Hospital, suffering from hypothermia, and he was dehydrated and covered with sores. Of course he'd been drinking. When he regained consciousness a week later, he denied having any family members. Anywhere.

"You've got to be kidding," said Joyce.

"After a few more weeks, they finally coaxed him into admitting he did have family — me — back in North Dakota."

"When had you last talked to him?" Bonnie asked.

"Six years ago."

"Oh my god," said Joyce. "What happened to him?"

I said he really *was* a psychologist but had lost his job seven years ago. He told Kaiser it was "early retirement." He'd worked for the California Veterans Health Administration in San Francisco. It took him about five years to run through the inheritance money from our parents who'd died twelve years earlier. He moved to Fairfield for cheaper rent. He lost that apartment, lost his car, and was left with only one possession, a bass fiddle he called Excalibur. He pawned it. Everything was gone, including his short-term memory. He was homeless for a year, with only the clothes he was wearing when he was picked up in the park.

"How does he live? *Where* does he live?" asked Joyce.

"He's now a ward of the state. He's got a two-hundred-dollar monthly pension from the Veterans Administration job. A little more from Social Security. After three months, supplemental security income came through. That pays for residential care at the Sunnyslope Board and Care Residence in San Mateo. They were the ones who asked me to come visit him."

"Dementia?" asked Bonnie.

"Sometimes. He's diabetic. He's got heart issues. And he's a drunk. Long-time."

"But he's so—I don't know—full of life!" Joyce was marveling at all the things I had marveled at over the years.

"His brain's on autopilot. Just don't ask him to make a choice. It will be wrong."

Bonnie touched her hand to her cheek. "He'll never get out of this board and care place or go to some place that's more...what, challenging?"

Just describing Nick's decline was challenging. I told them his first treatment program was at a geriatric convalescent home in San Francisco. He refused to take his insulin, he wouldn't get out of bed, he wouldn't brush his teeth or shave.

"So sad!" said Joyce.

"They said Nick should be in a more relaxed, less authoritarian, family-style residence, with live-in supervision. So, ten months ago he was moved to a board and care facility in San Mateo. Sunnyslope. He's doing much better, but it doesn't change the fact that he's on borrowed time."

"He's coming back," said Bonnie. I looked up to see Nick maneuvering awkwardly among the tables. He was patting down his strands of hair. With spit, I guessed.

"So you saw him today for the first time—in six years?" she asked.

"Well, twelve actually. My parents' funerals. The last phone call was six years ago. Yeah. I know. Neglect. Where's the brotherly love? But I'm here, now."

Joyce sipped her drink. "Well, we know what happened to him. What I'd like to know is what happened to you? You waited until this Sunnyslope called you even though you knew he almost died a year ago? Jesus!"

I was about to tell her none of her goddamn business when Nick arrived.

"Did I hear our Lord's name taken in vain? Hello, brother and lovely *frauleins*. What happened in my absence? Has my brother poisoned the ladies' good will by spreading untruths while I am about my ablutions?" He hung on to the back of his chair and burped. I was embarrassed. Nick wasn't.

"I told them about the last few months of your life. We were just getting into mine."

"Aha. I'm on the mend, and so will you be, brother, after my ministrations. How about another beer for ol' Nick on the occasion of his return from the john, not to mention our good luck at Stern Grove?" He lowered himself into his chair and made eyes at Joyce. I ordered him another non-alcoholic beer.

When it came, he looked at it dismissively and leaned forward. "So, Bonita. So, Joyce. Tell us about your relationship and leave nothing out that would help me help you."

The wine had unlocked Bonnie a bit. "You're funny," she said to Nick.

"He's nosy," Joyce said, frowning at Nick. "I am Bonnie's guardian angel."

"And her lover-in-waiting?" Nick shot back.

Joyce's frown turned to a glare. "*Au contraire*. Bonnie and I are hopelessly hetero, much to our chagrin when confronted with males with excess testosterone." I could see a battle of the Titans brewing.

"Yo there, mystery sister," Nick retorted. "I don't think we know about your status, Joyce. Bonnie's just out of the habit, Ben's a lifelong Latin teacher, I'm formerly homeless, and you...you are what?"

Joyce aimed her response at Nick: "Joyce is a single mother with three grown boys. And also a damn good realtor. I've been around the block." She gave us a sly smile before she sipped her wine. The bait of her brief vita lay on the table like a mousetrap.

Bonnie leaned forward. "We went to high school together. We were best friends."

"Back in the days when little white girls didn't bond with little Black girls," said Joyce. "But Bonnie came from wealth and my parents were mid-level professionals. Mother was a kindergarten teacher and father was a legal aid lawyer. She and I bonded."

"And stayed bonded," Bonnie said.

"Even when Bonnie entered the convent. She wrote me from the nunnery and told me about her decision. She was eighteen."

"Tell them about the application form," Bonnie said, her face reddening.

"Oh my god. The application form! After 'age' it asked for 'sex' and Bonnie said she figured they knew she would be female so she thought it meant 'ever had sex?'"

"I wrote 'never,'" Bonnie quickly added.

That made Nick beam. "I bet Mother Superior had an impure thought over that."

"Did she comment on your answer?" I asked.

"Never," Bonnie replied with a straight face.

I knew what was coming from Nick's mouth. "And today, if Doctor Nick asked you: 'Sex?'"

"Nick, lay off!" I bristled.

"Still never." She blushed deeply and her eyes watered up, as if only now she realized how invasive Nick's question was. I looked down. Joyce gave her some tissues.

"Never too late," Nick said in a cheery voice.

"Better later than earlier," Joyce rejoined, glaring at Nick. The waiter stood by our table.

We ordered off the menu, starting with warm popovers all around. Joyce had crab Louis, Bonnie the clam chowder, I had the halibut and Nick ordered a seafood omelet and a half-pound cheeseburger. Between bites, Nick regaled the women with his exploits around Half Moon Bay twenty-five years ago.

"Buttoned up Excalibur, my bass fiddle, packed him in the backseat of my Audi. Off we'd go for impromptu gigs at the smoky bars along Route One in the '70s. Plucking Excalibur until my fingers bled in the wee hours of the a.m. Always new guys, new sounds. Piano, horn, drums, bass."

"I could have accompanied you had we known each other," said Joyce. "I've kept up my piano lessons."

Nick went right on. "Sax. Guitar. And Excalibur. Bless his

long neck, yes sir. Bless that fiddle. You two are too young to remember the '70s."

"Oh Nick, we remember them well. They were good in so many ways," Bonnie said. I watched Joyce close her eyes.

"How good you will never know, sister," he cut her off. "You weren't there. We played the greats, the old favorites: 'How High the Moon,' 'Night and Day,' 'That Old Black Magic,' 'Oh, Lady Be Good.' I mean, you had to be there to understand what I'm saying. You know what I'm saying?" His fist hit the table.

Like a man who'd lost a limb but still moved as if to use it, Nick was developing quite a mood swing on non-alcoholic beer. He had been a mean, angry drunk. I checked the labels. Nick saw me watching him. He smiled with an "I-know-what-you're-thinking" grin. God Almighty, here he was with a pickled brain and he still could read my face. I wanted to whack him.

"Is the bro perplexed I'm getting louder? You do know, brother, that just thinking about the nearness of alcohol can spike levels of dopamine in the brain, generating those old feelings of joy. Dopamine in rats' brains soars when the little fellows are exposed to enough 'alcohol-related cues.' So that might be why ol' Nick is getting loud."

Nick ended his rant with a confidential nod to the women. "Ladies, life is all about the placebo effect."

I shook my head. "You've just seen a demonstration of why my brother and I have not talked to each other in six years!" My voice was controlled but I was furious.

"I feel like I'm kibitzing at a ping pong game," said Joyce. "Back and forth, crack, crack, the two of you batting away with dirty looks. You've been at it for a long time, even with a six-year break. Enough already."

I nodded. "How about some coffee? Nick is having coffee." I waved to the waiter, ordered coffee and asked for the check.

"We're paying for us," said Joyce. She put cash on the table. I made a move to pass it back to her, but she brushed my hand away.

"Wouldn't you rather owe us something?" asked Nick.

"I'd rather owe you zip," replied Joyce.

I scowled at Nick. He glowered back. "The kid brother wants me to go home sober and I insist on fucking up his plans."

I said, "How about not fucking up a nice evening? I say we let our friends go. They have somewhere to be at seven."

"They are rational adults, more than I can say for my fascist control freak of a brother! They can jump my scintillating ship of state if they want to. We don't have them on a ball and chain." He was getting louder. The waiter returned very quickly with coffee and at the same time presented the check.

"Why don't you come to my apartment for more coffee and dessert?" Bonnie said. I must have looked shocked. Joyce certainly did. What was Bonnie thinking?

"Will you excuse us?" Joyce stood. "Bathroom break." They retreated toward the restrooms. I figured they weren't coming back and I didn't blame them for dining and dashing. Outside, in the fading day, the seals flopped lethargically on the rocks. The waiter watched us from a few feet away.

Nick was in his own world. "What did I tell you, bro? I told you they wanted a little evening enjoyment. Sun goes down, antennae go up, the mating game begins. Nighttime revelry, right?"

I took a deep breath. "Joyce is right now telling Bonnie that she — Bonnie — is a little tipsy and needs to go home and go to bed and not get set up by a couple of guys she will never see again. Get a grip, Nick. Act your goddamn age."

"And who is going to set who up, bro? We're just a couple of harmless old fellows, right? Nothing like this in North Dakota, right?"

The women were back. Bonnie was smiling. Joyce's face was taut. "We'll go to my place for coffee. This is all Bonnie's idea. But you must leave by eight. And I'll throw you two out if you start fighting again."

"Capital," Nick shouted and stood unsteadily, then sat down quickly.

"Is that okay with you?" Bonnie asked me. She looked as shy and tentative as a little girl inviting the boy next door to a birthday party.

"Of course, Bonnie." It was the first time I had said her name. She smiled. "Oh, great!"

"We'll be on our way home at eight sharp," I assured her. "You don't have to worry about us camping out on Joyce's doorstep."

"How about camping in?" Nick growled. "I need time to counsel you two. What's the hurry?"

We all had drained our cups dry. "What Bonnie needs is not to rush into anything," Joyce said. "My friend is fresh out of the convent and I am her guide. I set the rules."

"And I ignore them when I choose to." Bonnie drilled the comment at her friend. "Joyce sometimes forgets that I am a middle-aged woman."

"Who...oh forget it. Let's go. Here's my address, Ben. A block from Saint Mary's Cathedral, on Gough Street near Geary. Can you find it?" Joyce handed me a slip of paper with a map on it.

"I'll find it," I said. "Can we bring something? Ice cream?"

"Some good dope?" Nick said.

"Just show up. I've got a full fridge."

"Disappointing," Nick said, shaking his head. "Well, I will bring a full set of nighttime games. I am the master of the revels at Elder Town." He stood and shook his hips suggestively. Bonnie just shook her head, trying to figure him out, I was sure.

Joyce looked exasperated with me. "Can you, will you, control your brother?" It was a demand, not a question.

"He's always tried and seldom succeeded!" he shouted and reached for Joyce's hand. He kissed it. As we left the restaurant, the waiter nodded an expression of pure relief.

"Oh, tomorrow, maybe you guys..." Bonnie stopped. She looked at Joyce. Joyce looked exasperated. I had the feeling Bonnie really wanted us over to her place, wherever that was.

"Why don't we just do tonight?" Joyce said icily.

"Ah, you have never experienced the revels of the night!" Nick suddenly shouted. He slurred the v of revels. It came out b.

"Who exactly are these rebels you keep talking about?" Joyce asked. "Good old boys from the south?" We were now at their car. Joyce was opening the driver's door. Bonnie had taken my arm.

Nick laughed. "Revels, not rebels, although I think Bonnie here is feeling rebellious, yes?"

"I'm feeling safe," she said quietly. She tightened her grip on my arm. "Please do come over." She let go, opened the passenger door and climbed in.

Joyce already had the shift in drive. She pulled out into the street and yelled back, "Thanks, gentlemen, for a nice time, in case you don't show."

"Honk if you love Jesus!" Nick yelled and waved his arms like a signal corpsman. Joyce honked and they were gone.

Now was the moment to correct the drift. Stern Grove I could understand: the thrill of the chase. Meet, greet, but then retreat. However, there followed The Cliff House rendezvous, the sharing of food and drink, the sharing of Nick's story and my face-saving late-in-life reunion with him. Then they saw me getting angry with him. I was embarrassed. That was supposed to be between him and me. These were the little ties that were starting to bind.

Stop by for a drink at Joyce's place? Bonnie invites us to something tomorrow? Whoa! Cut the string, correct the drift. Return immediately to Sunnyslope. Put Nick to bed. Call it a night and head to the B and B. Tomorrow or the next day for sure find out what I came to find out, whatever I could. Fly home. Savor the "nice time" with the ladies as a pleasant memory. No real damage done. Joyce had called off the chase, yes? "…in case you don't show."

He was shambling behind me. I heard a grunt, turned, and saw him falling backwards, like a boxer who'd been punched hard. He didn't try to ward off the impact. He just toppled and crashed on his back. I was terrified he had gashed the back of his head and we'd spend the next four hours in some ER. When I tried to lift him, he was dead weight. Finally, he grabbed my elbow. Excruciating minutes went by as he tried to get into a sitting position while I held his arms and pushed and pulled against his unsteady body. Then he was up. I felt for blood in his thin hair. There was none.

"What happened? Are you okay?" I was panicky. He was smiling.

"Bro, just lost my balance. Ready to rock. I'm unhurt, no thanks to that measly, non-alcohol piss water back there. Had there been real alcohol, I'd be flying!"

"Had there been real alcohol, you'd be flat on your ass in jail," I shouted.

Nick leaned back on the headrest. "On to Geary and Gough." Thank god he hadn't been drinking real beer. We didn't speak. A good sign, his silence. He might want to just sleep. I could return to Sunnyslope without him making a scene. But maybe he had had a concussion. Keeping him awake was the last thing I wanted to do. And if he needed a hospital, I'm close to one. So maybe we should go to Joyce's place, I told myself. He'd stay awake and we were minutes from a trauma center.

I took more than a few wrong turns, frequently consulting Joyce's map at red lights, and finally saw the white modernist banner-towers of the cathedral rising on the hill ahead of us on Geary and Gough streets. Joyce's condominium tower looked severely modern, like Joyce's style. And expensive, like Bonnie's clothes. I guessed Joyce had paid close to a million for her place. I followed her directions into the private garage underneath, parked, turned off the ignition, and bit my lip.

I could have backed out of the parking space. I could have pressed down on the gas pedal and driven him directly home. The truth was, it had been very seductive meeting these two women. I'd come to the bay area focused on a lonely, bruising interrogation of my sick brother, feeling sorry for myself all the way. That scenario was now scratched. Today's escapade was very exciting, very affirming. To be sixty-two years old and to be found interesting by two attractive women, well, that was heady stuff.

"You okay?" I asked Nick.

"Never been better," he shouted and got out of the car. "Get ready, bro. Watch me. The master of the revels."

We called up from a lobby that smelled of lavender and looked like serious money. Parquet floors, plush leather armchairs, tall floor lamps that emitted soothing light, beautifully framed watercolor paintings featuring San Francisco landmarks, high windows opening out to the street and the cathedral. Inhaling the lavender, I felt I was grasping the gold ring of upward mobility. Nothing like this in North Dakota.

Then we were in an elevator to the eighth floor and when the doors opened there in the hallway stood Joyce and Bonnie, looking terrific. They had changed from picnic outfits to cardigans, tank tops and pants.

Nick and I did not look terrific, what with Nick's fall in the parking lot and my wrestling him back up in his already scuffed-up clothing. Our damp-bottom chinos were now arguably lived-in. We belonged around a campfire.

"Okay, guys, come on in," said Joyce. She seemed a tad petulant, more like "Come on in, watch where you sit. The clock is ticking." Bonnie displayed no such reticence. She was smiling and seemed genuinely happy we had shown up. There would be no hugs yet. I had that awkward feeling I experience when I enter a stranger's house. Rave about the furniture? Smile at the host? Speak first or wait?

San Francisco has been called forty-nine square miles surrounded by reality. This apartment was nineteen hundred square feet surrounded by illusion. Nighttime San Francisco glowed outside the windows of the living room. I felt like I could reach out and touch the illuminated cathedral a block away.

The walls of the living room were covered with splashy modern art and gorgeous nature photographs. The sofas and chairs were slip covered in Marimekko, with hints of African tapestry. The wood-slat floors were buffed to a warm sheen.

"You have a beautiful home, Joyce," I said.

"Thank you."

Joyce showed us around. Nick was inspecting the place as if it were a crime scene. A half wall topped with potted ferns led into a dining area. A very elegant glass-top dinner table was surrounded by teak and bamboo chairs. Diners could gaze at the bay. We walked down a hallway that led to a kitchen with granite counters, white cupboards, and a massive butcher-block island in the center. Beyond the kitchen were two bedrooms, a guest bathroom and a small study.

It was one classy condominium. Nick and I were out-classed, but I was sure only I noticed it. Nick asked to use the bathroom. Joyce and Bonnie walked into the kitchen. I sat down in the living room.

I had hoped Joyce would serve coffee and nothing else. Nick came out of the bathroom and turned into the kitchen. I figured he was scouting for a beer in the refrigerator. The women sent him out empty-handed minutes later and he joined me in the living room. He gazed at the banner-towers of the cathedral and pronounced them "sterile."

"Who's sterile?" inquired Joyce, carrying a tray of cups. Bonnie followed with a coffee server.

"The beverage choices," replied Nick.

"Decaf, for the elders among us," quipped Joyce.

"No caffeine, no beer? So what the hell, let the games begin!" Nick shouted.

Whenever I had feared my brother was going to embarrass me, I would try to upstage him with a Latin translation. I did it now. *Ludi incipiant!* I said.

Bonnie laughed. "You really are a Latin teacher?"

"One of the best." She seemed genuinely interested. "Of course there are damn few of us left, so my claim is plausible."

"I had a wonderful Latin teacher. She was the one who suggested I join the convent. Sister Gloria. A beautiful woman. She was just ten years older than I was. Gloria left a year after I took vows. She married and now has grandchildren."

"*Sic transit gloria mundi*, right?" Nick chortled. "Gloria checked into the world."

Bonnie corrected him. "Thus passes the glory of the world."

Nick was stripping off his sweater. "I know, I know. For all of us the world's glory is transiting, tempus is *fugiting*. But your Gloria transited to sexual womanhood. She said, 'Stop the world, I want to get on! Now my question is, how do we get *elders* on the world?"

He started lecturing. "You think Elder Town is a day activity program, as they call it in the literature. Yes?"

"Who—or what—is Elder Town?" asked Joyce. "I thought you lived at a place called Sunnyslope."

Her eyes followed Nick. He was prowling the room, hands held behind his back. "Indeed I do live at a place called Sunnyslope," he said. "Sunnyslope Board and Care. I call it Sunnyslope I'm Bored and I Dare. The senior center is a place called Elder Town. Where elders get down during the day and sometimes all night! Bathroom break." He headed for the bathroom.

"Nick thinks he runs the program there," I said in my interpretive and interceptive role. "He talks about it like it's a nonstop orgy of group sex. Disregard ninety percent of it as fantasy." Silence for a minute or so.

"Can I pour myself a glass of water?" Nick yelled from the kitchen.

"Glasses are in the cupboard next to the frig." Joyce looked tense, ready to pounce on Nick if he started acting crazy. I did not blame her.

Nick returned. He shot me a mean look. "I heard you. Not

even my brother knows about the revels of the night. It is a paradigm-busting night activity program!"

"Okay, Nick," Joyce said. "Rebels. Revels. Schmevels. What happens at night? Just get the shock stuff out. Bonnie and I are grown girls, we...."

Nick's eyes always looked gorged when he got backtalk. I could almost feel his blood pressure rising. He pulled out a pack of cigarettes. Joyce glared at him: "Ah, Nick, no smoking here."

He turned and sauntered over to a sliding door, unlatched it and stepped out onto a small balcony. I figured we were about eighty feet up. He lit the cigarette. "How's this?"

He blew a puff of smoke out at the cathedral and hung over the thin railing. If he lost his balance as he did when he fell outside the Cliff House, he'd drop eighty feet. I froze.

"Nick, be careful. It's dark out there," Bonnie said.

"I am not responsible for him!" Joyce glared at me.

"But it's all about the night!" he shouted as he retreated from the railing. "I am the originator of the program here in Land's End on the West Coast of the US of A. I am Doctor Nick, the king of the sundowners." He faced us. "You know about the phenomenon of sundowning, right?"

The women looked at each other; Bonnie nodded her head a tentative yes. And Joyce said, "I've read something about it."

Nick blew smoke off the balcony and stabbed the air with his cigarette. "It's end-of-day anxiety, restlessness, confusion. Accompanies some forms of dementia, early stages of Alzheimer's." He took a quick puff and tossed the cigarette over the railing.

"I've taken the liberty to broaden the definition. We all experience some kind of anxiety around sundown as we get older. And it intensifies as we suffer cognitive deterioration. We get restless, anxious, all of us want to bay at the moon. As the sun sets, all the board and care, the assisted-living, the nursing homes across the country are popping downers down, down, down the throats of their cognitively deteriorating residents.

'Down, boys! Down, girls!' I call it the Down syndrome. But we don't want to go down! We want to *get* down!"

Bonnie sat, entranced. Joyce glared at me as Nick continued. "In our little bedrooms we can't sleep no matter how many downers we take. We are sleep deprived. You know about sleep deprivation. That's what sends people to nursing homes and booby hatches in the first place. We're confused—we're just out of surgery, or we're in new, unfamiliar surroundings. When we are institutionalized, we spend the day getting med, fed and bled. Then comes night, full of terrors—the psalmist knew it: 'I do not fear the terrors of the night nor the arrows that fly by day.' Well *we* fear them, Mister Psalmist, bet your blooming ass we do! We get anxious. We want to get up, roam the halls, bust out. But the great cornucopia of opiates and hypnotics poured into our trembling mouths stultify us."

A deep breath. He seemed supercharged and started a rap. "When the sun starts going down, the old folks really start to frown. Darkness is the worst of times. Darkness really screws our minds." He was snapping his fingers and shaking his hips.

"This is not SAD, seasonal affective disorder. SAD is the older brother. This is DAD, diurnal affective disorder. Getting dark outside means getting disoriented and discombobulated inside." He pointed to his brain. "Despite the downers we are still flying. The spirit wants to fly away, dance away from the darkening earth. You see? Down with downers, up with sundowner therapies." He headed for the railing again.

"Go for it, Nick. Drop eighty feet." Joyce held up her palms in a gesture of submission.

"Goddamnit, Nick, we're heading to Sunnyslope if you don't quit playing King Kong out there!" He heard the anger in my threat. He walked slowly back to the door.

"So what do you do about it?" asked Joyce in a calm voice. "People with dementia get antsy at night, so they get drugged and fall into bed quietly. Nothing new there, we have all heard about zombie-fication of old people." She folded her arms.

"Cynic!" Nick cried out, shaking a finger at her.

"So what is so therapeutic about your solution? Let them run wild? What are the nighttime rebels doing all night? Rebelling? Party on, everybody! Go to bed when you feel like it! It sounds like a frat house free-for-all." Joyce made a wrinkled face and shook her head.

Nick came inside and held out his arms as if embracing the world, not the three feet between him and Joyce. First his mouth muscles moved in exasperation. Then the words caught up with the mouth. "I start a nighttime revels program at Elder Town, that's what I do about it. That's spelled R-E-V-E-L-S. And the lovely Andrea gets the top brass at Elder Town to go along with it, to pay for it."

"Who's Andrea?" Joyce asked.

"The program director at Elder Town." He said each word slowly, distinctly, as if exasperated by his loutish audience.

"People get dressed and go out at night?" asked Bonnie.

"At seven p.m. the van comes to rouse the senior citizenry of San Mateo from their rest homes and nursing homes. Y'all come! Healthy elders, sick elders. The healthy ones help the sick ones. No anti-anxiety medications are allowed on this night. We gather at Elder Town. For the next twelve hours we paint, we pot, we dance, we are massaged, we listen to Mozart and Benny Goodman and the incomparable Ella Fitzgerald."

"Every night?" asked Joyce.

"Monthly, on the full moon if possible," replied Nick.

"You are joking, Nick," Bonnie said. "I can't imagine the state of California letting people out at night! What are their families paying for except security?"

He dismissed Bonnie with a wave of the hand. "Wrong, lovely Bonnie. Everything starts in California and fifty years later it's the norm in North Dakota." He pointed a smoke-stained finger at me. "Nothing like this in North Dakota—yet. Security might be number one in North Dakota nursing homes. Here in California, it's *bonhomie*."

Joyce leaned forward over her legs. "Okay, so this is allowed. This is a voluntary program, right? Nobody is forced to leave the security of their room, the safety of their assisted-living home. It's the adventurous, the risk-takers, and the ones with dementia that sign up. And then what happens? What actually happens to mad Sally or woozy Susie or roaring George? How do they handle sundowning any better than if they were drugged up at home?"

"Aha, wrong again! Sally, Susie, and George are normal red-blooded geezers and act like it. Not adventurous, not risk-takers. They are just ready for some action! Just as you would if you were in their shoes." He slipped closer to Joyce's face.

"My friend, is your life so different? You get into a routine, after a while you hate it. Your regular meals, your regular medications, your regular entertainments. You need a break, a breakout, so you go to Tahoe or Napa Valley or wherever. Your nightlife takes on frisson, yes? I am the master of frisson. How do you generate frisson, that moment of intense excitement in the lives of those living in this country's elder warehouses?" He stopped for a breath. "I will tell you! You rip away the medications we all rely on and you perk up for one brief shining all-nighter!" Nick tore an imaginary pill tray out of the hands of an imaginary nurse, strode back to the balcony and threw the imaginary contents over the balcony. "Out, out, damned rot!"

He returned inside. "The revels are Doctor Nick's old reliable placebo." He sounded each syllable slowly. "Plah-SEA-boh."

He started pacing. "We start slow. Annie hasn't been out of her chair in months, chin resting on breast. Dolores has been manic, roams the hallways. Aloysius dribbles on his shirt in front of the TV. So we start with meditation, 'Ohhhmmm.'" He motioned to us. "Do it please."

We started chanting. Nick waved his arms like an orchestra conductor pleading for more nuance.

"We get people in a good place. We arrange for a pack of pooches to be delivered. They ooze love and attention. And we're not talking just the spare bespittled hound from the Humane Society. We're talking twenty, thirty, forty pedigreed puppies. We are overwhelmed with love! Then we do arts and crafts at whatever level, from paper flower-making to wood-working. Sometimes we all go out: a late-night restaurant, now and then a traveling circus show. Back at ET by midnight and we storm the kitchen, where we have early-morn snacks, fruits, broccoli, cauliflower, cheeses, cold cuts. At one o'clock, we get down for a little blues music. Somebody from San Mateo volunteers to play the piano, and ol' Nick joins in with a rented bass fiddle. The disco ball starts spinning, the lights are lowered, the more able-bodied shake their booties, the less able-bodied shake their maracas. We make everybody who can walk get up and dance." He strode toward a stereo set.

"Joyce, put some music on for us, please."

Joyce got up, quietly flicked on the stereo and slid in a compact disk. Frank Sinatra started crooning. "I left my heart in San Francisco."

I started laughing. "Is it mandatory that that song be played at all hours and places in this town?"

"I'm trying to humor him," Joyce said, glaring at me. "In case you haven't noticed, your brother is frothing at the mouth."

Ignoring the commentary, Nick went to Bonnie, held out his hand and drew her to her feet. She blushed but didn't resist. "Let's say Bonnie is a resident who comes to night revels for the first time. The shades are pulled, the lighting comes on, the incense is lit. Fragrance invades the room. I say, 'Let's dance, sweetheart.' Bonnie resists. 'I'm not a floozy,' she protests."

"I'm not a floozy," Bonnie parroted. "I'm just out of the convent for goodness sake."

Good for you, I thought. Show a little impromptu spine before the dominator.

But of course the dominator went right on, "And then you say, 'And I have only half a right hip.' Say it."

Bonnie leaned a little to the left and let her shoulder drop. "And I have only half a left hip." Bonnie looked pleased with her impersonation.

"Whatever. I lead her to the floor, letting her rest her bad hip against mine. She starts shaking her torso ever so stiffly.

I touch her gently. Here." Nick put his hand just above her breasts.

"Watch out, he's putting the move on you," Joyce warned.

"Sometimes they forget to button their blouse," Nick groused as he removed his hand from Bonnie's chest and led her back to the couch.

I had squirmed throughout this. Nick pulled me up and pushed Bonnie and me together. Then he turned to Joyce and took her hand. And soon the four of us were dancing to old Blue Eyes. Damn, Nick might be nutty, but he was as mindful as a yoga master. I had no idea what he'd do next.

"Then what, Nick?" asked Joyce, the real watchdog here. She'd shaken off Nick and turned off Frankie. Bonnie and I untangled, and returned to the couch.

Nick retreated just past the door on the darkened balcony and lit another cigarette. "Then it's back to the shuffleboard room where they've set up cots," he whispered. "Lights low, shoes off. The aides massage our feet. The elders who are totally out of it rest their heads on tables, and the aides massage their backs and shoulders and heads. Sometimes the elders massage the aides—you know, empathy is a two-way street. The ladies touch one another's faces. Some of us talk dirty to each other. Who's trying to hump who back at assisted living? Who's getting a *little assisted loving?*"

Bonnie looked mesmerized by Nick's tale, eyes wide and unblinking. Joyce tapped her fingers on the sofa arm.

"They reminisce about long-ago love affairs, the men they remember, some fondly, some bitterly. The marriages, the divorces, the sex, the kids, the good times, the failures, the disappointments, the highs and lows. Some cry, others laugh, oh yes, at the pity of it all. When the last of us falls asleep, the aides turn off the lights. I try to bed the program director, the lovely Andrea. She eludes me."

Nick wandered back into the room, looking pleased with his lecture. He rested a haunch heavily on the edge of the couch where Bonnie and Joyce sat. "At seven in the morning we're up for coffee and Danish, breathing exercises, a little yoga, and then back home."

And then he made his move. "We are all sundowners, ladies. We all need some late-night delight. Can I, assisted by bro here, give you the ultimate massage?"

He was cuffing his hands, warming them up. I waited for Joyce to unplug the evening. She stood. "Hey, I think it's decision time. And here's what I've decided—tonight is a wrap."

Nick whimpered.

"Bonnie and I are going to Haydn's *Creation* tomorrow night at the cathedral at eight. You can join us if you're interested. If not, no problem. But right now Bonnie and I need a little girl-time."

Nick had tumbled down onto the sofa and stared up at her. "We have not even started the whole beautiful liberating turn-on of tactile therapy. You can't stop now," he whined as he put an unlit cigarette into his mouth.

"The hell they can't," I said. "Nick and I need a little boy-time. Good idea to call it a day."

Nick glared at me. "Anybody who calls it a day when night comes on deserves to suffer sundown." He stood and stomped out to the balcony.

"You're not being helpful, Nick," Joyce said. She took Bonnie's hand. They stood near the door. I joined them there. Nick held his position on the balcony. His cigarette drooped downward, as if in disbelief the evening was over.

I gestured toward the door. "We're out of here. It's almost nine and I'll get lost going back to San Mateo. We may not get there much before midnight."

Damn. Nick just spread his legs, posing like an urban gunslinger. "What you don't understand is that the midnight rule is only for nights when we don't have the sundowning program. I simply call up José and tell him this is a specially designated night. He says 'Okay' quicker than you can say '*muy bien*.'"

I knew he was losing steam. I said, "We're going and no 'fuck that noise' protesting." He stood there, the sullen master of interrupted revels. Joyce folded her arms and waited. Bonnie glanced at me, turned tentatively to Joyce, then back toward me.

"I'd like to give you my phone number before you go," she announced. "If you want to call me, I'd love to have coffee tomorrow." She reached for her purse, pulled out a piece of paper and scribbled numbers on it. "Here." She handed it to me. I took it, folded it neatly, and placed it in my billfold.

"Thanks, Bonnie." I reached out for her shoulders and she sort of fell into me. It was a grand hug. I let go. Nick watched the scene, eyes flashing. This was surreal. She wanted to have coffee tomorrow. Nick wanted to seduce her tonight.

"Another bathroom and water break." He moved quickly down the hallway. The three of us waited silently. He finally returned and went right back to the balcony.

I glanced at Joyce and grimaced. I needed help. Joyce went out to the balcony and friendly but firmly took his arm. She led him to the door. He growled mildly all the way into the hall-way. She leaned over and kissed him on the cheek.

"'Night, Nick. It's been a swell day," she said.

"Really nice, yes, thanks so much," said Bonnie. She let Nick hug her. Nick hung on to her elbows and shook his head—a practiced gesture that said, too bad, lady, you're missing the biggest erotic charge that life can offer.

He snapped his fingers above his head like a tango dancer. "Remember the feelings I create. Frisson." He clicked his shoes. "Olé!"

When we reached the elevator, Nick turned and leaned against the wall. His face was five inches from Joyce's. " I think we need to talk about your sexual panic syndrome."

"I'd love to, but not tonight. Maybe tomorrow. But if you are in the market for a house, here's my card." She handed it to me. It gave her name and the real estate company information. No picture. Very discreet. Then the elevator doors opened. I stepped inside.

Nick sauntered in with a sashaying gait. "Ladies, your love boat is sailing off forever," he stage-whispered.

"Happy trails!" Joyce replied breezily.

"Goodnight, and thanks," I said as the door closed. I envisioned Joyce screaming in relief as we descended to the garage.

"Never put off until tomorrow what you can do tonight," he said to the four walls of the elevator. "We were so close! Bro, you blew the big Kahuna. I could have been a contender up there. Joyce is a classic case of frigidity. Maybe it's the white-black thing. Maybe I don't want to go there. Maybe she picks up men, turns them on and sends them packing. Dangerous business."

She picked the men up but was immediately cold and dismissive

I waited a few seconds, desperately courting calm. "Or maybe she just wanted to show Bonnie how it's done—you know, that you don't have to hop in bed the first night with the first guy you meet. Especially a raving mad guy!"

"Don't short-change yourself. Look, Bonnie's ready. Bonnie's been ready a long time."

"I think we call off this little caper right now. Let's go to Big Sur tomorrow."

I slid the van out of the garage and started looking for Highway 101 signs. Nick was trash talking a mile a minute. What could I take as real? What was delusional? And what did it matter what he wanted to do? He was a ward of the state and dependent on others for sustenance, health, wheels. What difference did it make?

Okay. It made a small difference. He was my brother still. Incontinent, incompetent, inconsiderate, still my brother. And he might still know what I wanted to know. Must attention be paid to this guy? Whatever is owed, whatever is needed to get at the truth. Nothing more.

Instead of looking for Highway 101, I took city streets, thinking I could wear him out while we drove past bars and clubs. "That looks like action central, that Brit's Pub there," he yelled. He shouted every time we passed another place. So many possibilities. So little cooperation from me.

We got lost. I just kept driving south until I saw a Highway 101 sign. Nick's head started drooping and he slept until we reached San Mateo.

Outside Sunnyslope, Nick came to and climbed out of the van. Barney and Arnie sat smoking on the patio. He kicked their chairs. "Hello, mates. Been getting any?" Both of them grinned and inhaled.

It was almost midnight. José let us in and showed me to a bathroom. I heard Nick say, "My brother is not used to San Francisco. He's a Bismarck boy where a late night is watching the ten o'clock news and midnight is a brief up and down for the nocturnal piss." José said nothing.

Nick walked outside with me and gave me a bear hug. "All right, bro, I'll have a few smokes with the lads. How about tomorrow?"

"I'll be here."

"No Bonnie?"

"I'll be here. Where do you want to go?"

"Big Sur. Shall we invite the girls?"

I laughed. "The girls." Like a pair of old guys talking about their wives. "Nick, Joyce has a job. It's Monday. I'll bet Bonnie works too. Tomorrow night, Haydn, remember?"

"Didn't Bonnie give you her phone number?"

"I'll call her in the morning. Goodnight, Nick."

"Don't blow this one," he shouted as I wheeled the van around. *Me* blow it? Nick had already blown the night to kingdom come.

All the way back to Palm Avenue and my B&B, I kept breathing deeply so I could sort things out. Wrap them up tomorrow for sure. A brief phone call should do it. I'll call Bonnie. She needed closure and best wishes. Joyce would be relieved. She needed us to get out of her life.

On the other hand, these two women were fun. Bonnie had a crush on me, but she'd recover fast. Joyce was no child. Why not include them in my business? They'd keep me sane, and they'd keep Nick's *id* from erupting.

The last two hours showed what I feared about coming here. Nick was chaos on wheels. He infuriated me with his mad talk of liberating others while he himself was desperate for alcohol and dope. The world's biggest disconnect was the distance between reality and illusion in my brother's mind. I was not going to make any changes in his life in the few days I was there, especially in my resentful state. But it wouldn't hurt if these two women gave Nick a spoonful of honey to offset the gallon of vinegar I was going to force-feed him.

I called Bonnie the next morning. Because it's what I do, I built a rationale: She's good for Nick. And I don't live here. Maybe a bond between the three of them will develop. Nick would have no-nonsense friends to visit him, take him out for lunch—on me—and generally rein him in. These women might be just what Nick needed.

I dialed her number slowly, ten seconds on each digit. The last thing I needed was a rush romance with an ex-nun in San Francisco. I was a widower. My wife had died six years ago. I was in my early sixties and was still helping pay off my kids' college loans. Not to mention thinking about retirement.

My kids. When they ask me what happened on this trip between me and their Uncle Nick, what will I tell them? We picked up two women? They'd want to know why he'd said he had no relatives, why he fell into that degree of separation. They'd want to know about him and me being reconciled. If I tell them about Joyce and Bonnie, they'll say, "What's with the two women, dad? Did you need a crutch to deal with your brother?"

All right, a crutch. With Bonnie and Joyce, I was just taking the easy way out, the same old guys' game: two men who can't say or do anything personal without a woman or two to help them say or do it. So be it. Why not the easy way? Maybe these women were using Nick and me to meet their needs. Bonnie was adjusting to life outside the convent. But Joyce? She seemed pretty happy with her life the way it was. These were two smart cookies who knew we were all at the age where usefulness was a step above sexual attraction. But useful in what way? What could they possibly want from this imbroglio?

José told me that Nick and the Sunnyslope residents were tied up until afternoon getting flu shots. My morning was free. No Big Sur today. I finished dialing and told Bonnie I'd love to meet her and Joyce for a late breakfast. She said Joyce was working, so it would just be the two of us.

Pause.

"Sounds good," I said, hesitating a few seconds too long.

"Are you sure?"

"Of course."

Coffee with Bonnie was just a little morning excitement. No hanky-panky. I was disappointed Joyce wouldn't be there. I liked her humor, her mouthy assertiveness.

Bonnie suggested a bakery in the Mission district not too far from her apartment. When I finally found it, I was fifteen minutes late. She was standing outside the bakery, waiting in a line of customers. She wore a long black and white checked skirt and a frilly white blouse under a pink sweater. She looked great. I was no fashion expert but I knew money was not a factor in her wardrobe choices.

"Hi," I said. "Your directions were great but I got lost anyway. Sorry I'm late."

She just smiled. "Hello, Ben. I'm so glad you could make time for coffee." She grabbed my hand.

"Time is what I have. Nick's got to have a flu shot. He and the Sunnyslope boarders are at a clinic until early afternoon."

"Still, it's a long way into town. This place is popular. I think you'll like it. The morning buns are to die for."

In line we chatted about Princess Diana's death—Bonnie said she adored Di and had cried hard over the news. I told her I sympathized with the Queen. We talked about the Burning

48

Man event now underway in the Black Rock Desert of Nevada. I hadn't heard of it. She described it as the ultimate counterculture event and said she had wanted to attend, but was happy now she hadn't—that sentiment accompanied by a look and a wink at me.

Once inside we found a corner table with our coffee, quiche and morning bun. I hadn't been out with a woman since…well, in a long time. My dissonance bell rang. What am I doing in this picture? I'm going back to Bismarck to prep my syllabus on Virgil's *Aeneid* for my loyal students who were still subjecting themselves to conjugating Latin verbs after three years of the stuff.

My juxtaposing Virgil's epic with Bonnie's mysterious agenda made me jumpy. Why? Of course: Dido.

"What? What are you thinking?" She looked very curious.

"Um, nothing. Well, I have been thinking about the *Aeneid*, which I am about to start teaching to my fourth-year Latin students. I'm thinking about Dido, the tragic queen of Carthage in North Africa. You remember Dido? *Sunt lacrimae rerum*, right?" I was being a pedantic jerk.

Her smile remained constant. "Dido meets Aeneas, girl meets boy, girl falls head over heels for boy, boy leaves girl behind. Girl kills herself."

I asked her, "How would *you* translate *"Sunt lacrimae rerum?"* These famous lines from the *Aeneid* were spoken by Aeneas as he discovered artwork commemorating the destruction of his beloved Troy. He was awestruck that Carthage, so far from the Trojan War, could shed such tears for the besieged city.

Bonnie recited the line confidently. "'Even here you can find tears for the suffering of others. Even here misfortune melts the heart.'"

Not exactly Virgilian hexameter but close enough. I sat with sticky bun residue all around my mouth.

She folded her arms on the table and got right to the point. "Ben, I am no Dido and you are no Aeneas. I knew what was going on yesterday at Stern Grove. I knew you were chaperoning Nick. Everything about Nick screamed 'in-patient out for the day.' That's why I encouraged Joyce to slide down into you. I wanted to meet a man who was caring for his brother or his friend or whoever Nick was, doing something beautiful and meaningful." She laughed. "I guess we were pretty obvious, huh?"

"We were flattered. I was, at least. Nick sees himself as a sexual magnet. He dragged her down." She laughed.

Observing me closely, she repeated the line: "'Even here you can find tears for the suffering of others. Even here misfortune melts the heart.'"

I felt hot, uncomfortable. She was lionizing me.

"Yes?" She cocked her head a little to the side.

I sipped my coffee and started to reply, but....

"I'm not coming on to you, Ben. I just...I want to make the most of this serendipity, this Stern Grove lark. And I think Joyce does too."

"It is a lark, yeah. I agree. Fun. Until Nick decides otherwise. As he did last night."

"Nick is part of it for me. I just left a life where I had vowed stability and obedience. Nick is all about instability and breaking rules. I love dealing with that." She laughed, as if startled by her new awareness. "I love my freedom, Ben. Maybe I'm in love with the freedom to do as I please. To chase a lark."

"Trouble with larks is that they end," I said in my best mock-solemn tone. "Accidental friends for a day. I'm leaving in two days and Nick's back in his assisted-living residence."

"Sunnyslope Board and Care." She was looking at me, wide-eyed, nodding her head yes, mentally spinning everything I said into her gauzy little lark.

"He doesn't have long to live," I said. "And I won't be back until the staff tells me he's slipping away."

"Don't worry. I just want to enjoy both of you. To me, you two are larger than life. That's enough."

"Bonnie, whoa, slow down. This may be a lark to you, but it's no caper. He's...."

"I know!" she whispered. "I want to be a little part of your time with Nick. You two are a gift to me. Whatever and whoever you are, I just want to be around the two of you. It's the nicest thing to happen to me in a while. It was all so spontaneous yesterday. And it will be over soon. Meanwhile I want to seize this day. *Carpe diem*, yes?"

We sat there quietly for a few seconds. She looked around the restaurant, then at me. "I repeat. I am no Dido. You are no Aeneas. This is no tragedy. It's a circus. 'Damn everything but the circus,' e. e. cummings told us. I want to clown with you and Nick."

Customers were standing nearby, waiting for a table. She stood and beckoned to a young couple hovering close to our table. When we left the restaurant, she took my arm as we walked. Her look was ecstatic. A woman about her age approached us and smiled.

"Where's your car?" I asked her.

"I walked. Will you give me a ride back?"

"Sure."

When we reached the van, I opened her door and she got in and reached over to unlock my door. I had not seen that since the 1970s. I used to love that little routine about girls. She stayed leaning over and kissed my cheek, and then she sat back, buckled up and closed her eyes.

"So, we want you to come with us to the Hayden concert at the cathedral tonight. At eight. Joyce took some convincing, but I'd *really* like it if you'd come." Her voice trembled as she said, "Will you?"

"It sounds fantastic, but I don't know if Nick is up to it. You saw him last night. I've not seen him in a big public setting. He may freak out."

Bonnie opened her eyes and stared straight ahead. "He'll be fine. Please?"

I nodded yes.

She smiled and gazed out the window as we drove up her street, a steep, winding little avenue named Saturn Street. I could understand why she'd want a ride home.

"This is such fun. You know? I have no agenda, really. Just an ex-nun out for fun. Besides, I'd have to justify a relationship to my brothers. I grew up with three brothers, the only girl. Those guys always loved me so much. Too much. They made sure my high school dates were good guys. When I joined the convent, they breathed easy for years. But ever since I left, one or the other of them calls me every day. 'Bonnie, you okay? You dating anybody? You want to talk to any of us, call day or night. Watch out, there are so many divorced jerks out there looking for one-nighters. You call us, okay?' Joyce and my brothers—my vigilant minders."

The van ground gears as it chugged up the last vertical stretch of Saturn. I stopped in front of a cute, green Victorian. I put the car in park.

She opened her door, then turned to me. "So it's not good-bye." She got out, walked to the sidewalk and smiled back at me. "Haydn, then, tonight. We'll meet you at the church." I waved at her. She waved back and walked into her apartment.

A really nice woman. Trusting, no guile. But it was time to get down to business. I was in San Francisco because a great big impersonal health care system tracked me down and said you've got a brother out here who almost died on the streets. And a small board and care place called me later—"Shouldn't you want to see him?" Okay, I did show up, ten months later, at the end of summer, just as school was about to start. I'm here.

I sped south to San Mateo. Talk about having an agenda. Bonnie and Joyce were starting to scuttle my agenda of an in-and-out visit and getting some quick answers from Nick to the question I'd agonized over for six years. There was something about Bonnie that reminded me of my dead wife. The naiveté, the openness—my wife's sympathy for Nick in the years I'd lost touch with him. I never wanted to ride that rollercoaster again.

Okay, this is just a lark. Go with the flow one more time. Haydn tonight.

"Well, bro, thought you'd never show up. Did you get some action last night after dumping ol' Nick?" He was on the front porch with the gang: Barney, Arnie and Rudy, the medicated men of Sunnyslope. What had they been like in younger years? Had they led reasonably contented lives? Had their wives? Had they beat their wives? Did anyone ever come to visit them now, other than an occasional church volunteer or a caseworker from some agency? Like Nick, did they have a sibling who shunned them? Why? They were quietly smoking and staring at the horizon—or somewhere far away— while Nick talked. I had left Bonnie an hour ago.

"I slept at the bed and breakfast. Alone. I had breakfast with Bonnie."

Nick's eyes widened. "Right. No sex. And Arnie here performed open-heart surgery on Barney and Rudy this morning. You must have gotten...."

"That was all pretty intense yesterday. Maybe we can dial down the drama tonight."

"Tonight?"

"We are invited to join them at St. Mary's Cathedral."

"How so?"

"For a concert: Haydn's *Creation*."

That was not Nick's idea of fun. "And afterwards?"

"Nothing definite. I'm sure we'll do something fun. Joyce is organized."

"Goddamn control freak is what Joyce is," Nick sputtered.

want to know more about
these characters

Rudy blinked. Arnie coughed. Barney grinned.

"Shut up!" Nick yelled at the three of them. "I'm casting pearls in front of three swine."

"Easy does it, Nick. Your mates are enjoying themselves."

"Fuck that noise."

"Let's go. Is that the best you've got to wear?" He was wearing a washed-out, white cotton pullover with a v-neck that had been mercilessly laundered into a yellowing u-neck. I felt bad as soon as I said it. His shirt and pants were clean, after all. I just didn't want him looking like a bum.

"You're right. We're going to the house of God. I should look good for him and the two of them. How about the jacket of many colors you sent me in the mail?"

I was moved. I had sent him the jacket a dozen years or so ago. "You've still got it?"

"Yo, bro. It somehow stayed with me through thick and thin all the way here to Sunnyslope. I'll get it." He opened the door and went in. Pay the guy a compliment when he returns, I told myself.

José came out. "Hi, Ben. You taking him out again? You got lots of energy, man."

I told José where we were going and that it would probably be late again. "It's okay," he replied. "Nick, he stays up late most nights listening to music. We make him listen down in the basement so Barney can sleep. He *loves* the night, that guy."

"So it's all true, he goes to Elder Town at night and comes home early in the morning?"

"Once a month. Sundown night. He tells us at breakfast how many ladies he took to bed. My sisters blush. I just laugh. I think they watch TV there all night long. But he's a character, man."

I found his assessment of Nick pretty accurate. Talk the good game, brag about sexual conquests. Pretty soon the listener doesn't know what to believe. One day here, and it was already happening, me getting more and more ungrounded with Nick, surely the most deluded psychologist in the profession.

Nick returned, wearing the jacket. It was a mail order fleece jacket—a crazy quilt of patterns and hues, reds and greens, oranges and blues. I had never seen him in it. I was amazed it had survived his falling down in Golden Gate Park as paramedics struggled to get at his skin for an IV needle. He looked good in it. It distracted from his worn chinos and chafed running shoes. He'd even combed his hair.

The compliment: "Nick, you look great. Right out of GQ."

He pounded his chest. "Behold, Suleiman the Man! The Emperor of Eros!"

"Like I said, a real character, your brother," laughed José.

Now this guy José, this stocky Mexican-American with dark hair, he was the real thing, a caretaker. "José, how do you put up with this stuff?" He shrugged and smiled as if to say just part of his job description. I looked at Barney, Arnie and Rudy, all of whom were studying Nick with vacant stares. Barney wore the hint of a smile. Nick and I walked to the van, and as we drove off, we waved at them all. Barney waved back, or maybe he was batting a fly. It was three in the afternoon.

"Nick, let's go to Golden Gate Park.

He gave me a look. "Why not Big Sur?"

"How about Big Sur tomorrow?" I wanted to know more about where they found him. "Do you remember what happened when they found you in the park?"

"Oh, man, you think I can remember that? It's all a blank. But hey, I was wearing this jacket!"

We drove up Highway 101, into the city. I'd mapped out directions to Haight Street, which turned out to be not that far from Bonnie's place. Nick had hung out on Haight Street during the day, and then ended up in the park at night. Maybe he'd recognize a building or a favorite place to sleep, or better yet, we might meet someone who'd remember him. We'd talk to the bartenders, the locals, and see if any of them knew Nick. Had he been mugged? Arrested? Had he exposed himself? Been caught shoplifting? What had happened to him?

For six years I had chosen not to know what was happening to Nick. I always changed the subject when my daughters asked about their Uncle Nick. He's doing his thing, we're doing ours. Frances and Clare had long since become adults, and here I was, mucking about, a year after his near-death, ambivalent at best, compressing the last days of Uncle Nick into the three days I'd given myself. I knew if I didn't find out the truth, one of my kids would take it on as a personal obligation. But Nick would be dead. And I'd be a resentful old man.

No wonder Nick told the Kaiser people he had no family. Here's how: I'd left him no option. My fury had built a wall between us. A wall of mutual disownment. I'd given myself three days to own up to the past. Thinking about it now, I realized it wasn't a very generous offer.

The social workers at Kaiser found out he lost his job at the V.A. about seven years ago. Three years ago he'd moved to a town called Fairfield, halfway to Sacramento. Then what? When did he end up on the streets?

Maybe we'd find a drifter, a shop owner, a bartender who remembered him. Maybe somebody knew one of his old friends. Or maybe I'd get a break and Nick would start to remember something important.

I knew he was a regular at a drop-in center on Haight Street. The staff there had been in touch with the county and helped create a small file on Nick. The drop-in center was not too far from the park. Nick liked to keep things close. For a wanderer, he never wandered far. His life was contained in a single street within two blocks of Golden Gate Park. He would have been easy to find back then.

I parked the van outside the drop-in center. I'd seen psychedelic art before, but none to match the kaleidoscopic scene on the façade of the building next-door. An image of a snarling black she-wolf guarded the door, which was so covered with concentric circles and hallucinatory figures I couldn't see a doorknob. Nick got out and headed for the colorful door until I tugged at his sleeve and guided him back to the plain old storefront that housed the drop-in center. He stood on the sidewalk and vigorously scratched his eyebrows. He saw the name of the place on a window.

He turned and looked at me. "Where the hell are we? Am I supposed to know this place?"

"You were a frequent visitor here."

"When?"

"Last time was about a year ago. Before they found you in the park. In a coma."

"Outstanding detective work, bro!"

"You were homeless two years ago, and you came here for food and a shower and some time off the street."

"Who says so?"

"San Francisco County Human Services."

"Let's go in. Maybe I'll recognize the innkeeper."

Just then a guy of indeterminate age came out the door. Matted hair, missing teeth, patchy whiskers, shirt open to the navel. Like I imagined Nick a year ago. He sidestepped out of our way and lurched as if to hit one of us before rambling off. I grabbed the door and held it open for Nick.

It was dark inside. All the lighting came from floor lamps. No drab ceiling lights. Just a dozen people splayed out on couches and chairs, and drinking coffee in foam cups. The room was spotless though.

"Can I help you?" a young woman said as she approached us.

"I'm Doctor Nick."

"Nice to meet you, Doctor." She turned to me.

"I'm his brother. Ben."

"Hi, Ben. I'm Katie. So would you guys like a little coffee?"

Nick held up his hand. "Actually, Miss Katie, my brother seems to think I once was a frequent guest here. Do you recognize me?" He actually posed for her; first a frontal view, then a profile. Katie smiled, studied his face, looked at me, and then back at Nick.

"I've only been here two months. When's the last time you were here?"

"About a year ago," I said.

"I could ask Jennie. She's been here three years."

"That would be great," I said. The pungent odor of used clothing was strong. Katie returned with a stout woman somewhere in her forties. She recognized Nick the second she saw him.

"Hi there, Doctor Nick. How are you?"

Bingo.

"And you are...?" He studied her nervously. "Have I counseled you?"

She laughed. "No, no. I'm Jennie. I referred people to you."

"Have we ever fucked?"

"Geez, Nick," I blurted out.

"Not likely," Jennie said.

"Name a client."

She pointed across the room to a man in his late sixties. His shock of white hair gave him the aura of a dazed, immobilized Einstein. Wrapped in a red blanket, the man lay sunken in an old, overstuffed armchair. He'd been sleeping. Jennie went up to him and ruffled his hair.

"Gorgeous George, you recognize Doctor Nick?" The man sat up, pushed back the hair from his face and peered at Nick.

He smiled wearily. "Hey, Doc. Been getting any?"

Jennie grinned. "See, Nick. You're a legend."

Nick was pleased with the recognition. With a brain lesioned by a thousand licks of dope, he truly did not know where he was, but "been getting any?" always rang a bell for him.

"Not in recent months," Nick said, a bit despondently.

Nick wanted to go. I wanted to talk to the man. I walked over to him, to the beat of the Spice Girls' "Spice Up Your Life" coming from a second-hand boom box. Didn't take much to imagine Gorgeous George and Nick interrupting the center's calm with a shout fest.

"Hi, George. I'm Nick's brother, Ben."

"Hi, Ben. You been getting any?"

I couldn't help but laugh. "Afraid not. George, wonder if you can help us. We're trying to piece together what happened to Nick."

Gorgeous George scratched his head. "Let's see. He told me he was the best goddamn doctor in the Bay Area. And, oh yeah, he said he had scored with more women than anyone in the history of…" He thought for a moment. "…scoring. Yeah, that's what he said—and often."

"All true," said Nick, who had clasped his hands behind his back in professorial style.

"I used to win Einstein look-alike contests every year until they got tired of giving me free movie tickets. I got depressed after I was told I couldn't enter anymore. Doctor Nick helped me deal with it."

This was the extent of George's contribution. I thanked him.

I turned back to Jennie. "Any memories of my brother?"

"Oh, yeah," she laughed. "He used to have an office here." She couldn't resist air quotes. "A little closet over in the corner. He'd see male guests in there. We didn't let women in there alone with him."

"He actually helped people?"

"Oh yeah," she replied. "He could talk the lingo, and he had good words for anyone who was focused enough to listen to him. He was prescribing "meds" for anyone who would ask."

I could hear the air quotes around the word meds.

"He'd fill little bottles with candy." She turned to him. "I'm glad to see you still standing, buddy."

"I'm indestructible."

"You definitely are." She turned back to me. "He used to get food at McDonald's down the street. Ask for the manager. He's a good guy."

"Where would he have bought beer?"

"Before you get to McDonald's, toward the park. There's a little off-sale place called Danny's. Danny'll remember Nick."

I thanked her. We walked out onto Haight Street and continued toward Golden Gate Park. Danny's storefront window was filled with large signs featuring special buys spelled out in garish lettering. I led Nick inside. It was a tiny shop. The shelves were stocked with six-packs of beer and some cheap wine. Packaged snacks and mammoth plastic soft drink bottles were positioned near the cash register. Nick perked up.

"Doctor Nick, how the hell are you?" The heavy guy behind the counter in jeans and t-shirt and an apron had to be Danny. "You been in Mexico? Florida? On a cruise? I've missed you, buddy." Nick on a cruise. Ha! Nick wasn't registering. "Hey, Nick, it's Danny!"

"Hey, Danny," said Nick.

I introduced myself. "Nick's been in the hospital and is still a little disoriented about his time here."

Danny stepped back and surveyed the two of us, me especially. I realized he had no idea who I, Nick's buddy, was. He looked me over a couple of times.

"Brother?" he asked. He looked at Nick for confirmation.

"My brother from Bismarck, Enn-Dee," Nick answered.

Danny was satisfied. "Well, Nick was a good customer. He didn't have a lot of ready cash but he always paid. It was rough out there, you know? He had to be careful."

"Did he ever get rolled?"

Danny looked at me and then at Nick. "Ever get rolled, Nick? I don't think so." Nick reached for a six-pack of Sam Adams. The question caught his attention.

"Hell, no. But I think I've bought beer here."

"Sure did," Danny avowed. "You were a gentleman in here. If somebody got belligerent with you, you just flustered them with your psycho-talk."

I figured Danny was only telling half the story, protecting his small business. "Thanks, Danny."

"How about a six-pack of Sam Adams?" asked Nick, who had dropped the package on the counter. Danny eyeballed me.

"Not today, brother." I winked at Danny and we left. Nick shot me his usual dirty look.

We had less than a block to the park when I saw the golden arches. "Recognize it?" I asked.

"Indeed I do." He quickened his pace. It was the last business place before Stanyan Street and the park. A couple of street people were propped up on the front steps. Both had ageless skin stretched over skeletal protrusions of bone. Everything about them—skin, hair, eyes—all the color of bronze. They could have been in their thirties or their seventies. I had no idea.

"Excuse us, please," I said, hoping they'd move to let us pass. They didn't budge.

Nick sized them up. "We'd like to get by." They didn't move a muscle. We climbed over them and walked into McDonald's.

"I've been here before. But damned if I know when." He surveyed the tables and examined the occupants, who were mostly replicas of the two on the steps outside.

I walked up to the counter. "Is the manager here?"

"Sure. Mr. Flores?" he said, turning to the short, pleasant-looking man behind him.

"Hi, Nick. How's it going?" he asked when he walked toward us.

"Good, good. Do I know you?"

"Hugo, Hugo Flores. You forgot me already?"

"'Fraid so, hombre. Can I have a Big Mac and a coke?"

"Always a charmer," I said, looking at Hugo, surprising myself I'd said it out loud.

Hugo laughed. "Sure, Nick." He motioned to one of the young counter people to fix Nick up.

"You a relative?" He smiled at me.

"A brother. Nick's forgotten most of the last two years. Can you tell us anything?"

He looked back at Nick. "You were here every day for, gosh, at least a year or so, right up until about a year ago."

He chuckled. "You were very well behaved—except when you weren't!

Nick chuckled.

"You lived in that cluster of trees over there. Remember?" He pointed to the park. Then he turned to me. "Nick said he never wanted to be far from the action, from safety in the forest. He called the park the 'forest prime-evil' or something like that.

"Yes, the forest primeval," Nick said. "Noble savages all of us."

"He talked a lot of my customers down from hallucinations in here, I can tell you that. So he ate whatever he wanted, no charge. Yeah, we miss Nick around here." Nick munched the Big Mac and drank the soda that Hugo had poured for him. "You okay, Nick?"

"I can see daylight," Nick answered between bites.

"He's in a place called the Sunnyslope in San Mateo," I said. "Life's pretty good now for him."

Hugo kept talking, for my benefit, I could tell. "Every day Nick showed up like around two in the afternoon." He took Nick's arm. "We fixed up a little table tent for you, on that table right over there. The sign said, 'The Doctor is in.' Even customers who weren't stoned or high liked to talk to you and tell you their troubles." He turned back to me. "They gave him little bits of money now and again. Not a good idea, I suppose. Nick liked beer and dope." Now he looked at Nick. "And then one day you didn't show up." Nick was listening in an absent way, eyeballing the customers, a seller looking for a buyer.

I gave Mr. Flores a ten-dollar bill. He pushed it away. "Thanks," I said. "For everything."

He smiled and put a hand on Nick's shoulder. "You behave now, Doctor Nick. Come see us again." He was the right manager for this place.

We crossed Stanyan Street. The forest primeval beckoned. Tall, gnarled old trees framed a deep and wide expanse of green beyond. We walked through a fountain plaza packed with college-age kids, sagging under dirty backpacks. Some paths led up a hill, others aimed for the park perimeter. I fought the instinct to stay near the perimeter, near streets where there were tourists, and locals strolling, jogging, walking their dogs. We chose the path that led up the hill.

There, under sheltering trees, lay scattered circles of more bronzed people who looked frozen in repose on torn blankets and greasy bedrolls, waiting for passersby to drop some coins onto the ground, as payment for the privilege of gawking.

"Sun down, sun up, these citizens are good people!" Nick exclaimed.

"Recognize anyone?" I asked him.

"I recognize fellow travelers on the road of life."

We walked to an unoccupied grove and sat down on the grass. Nick had made his last stand somewhere nearby. I could feel it. "Look familiar?" I asked.

He scooped up some dirt and flung it away. "A joint would be nice right about now. Lying on my back, looking up at the sky."

"You remember anything about this place? The cops found you in this park in a diabetic coma. You were close to dying. You might have been lying right here." I scratched some dirt near me. "Maybe you left something here, a pencil, glasses."

Nick sighed. "Just the forest."

"Goddamnit, you almost died here!"

"You always saw the trees and not the forest." He was angry, really angry, and went right on talking. "We all die somewhere. I see the forest, the *sitz im leben*, the whole fucking context. You're looking for a place, a piece of earth that has coordinates, but not context. Life is *all* context, bro. Lock onto it. Live it!"

I backed off. Our realities were a world apart. I could almost feel his brain cells floating away from their lobes, like icebergs calving off a glacier. And I could feel the great gaps left behind.

I decided to deflect. "When you lost the apartment in Fairfield, where did you go?"

"Always westward."

I pressed him. "San Francisco. They said...."

"Who is this 'they'? Who's following me?" He looked really angry again.

"The county. You went to a shelter. You stayed maybe a week. Then you left. You came here and lived in the park. You ate at McDonald's across the street. You drank whatever you could bum off others or earned by talking. And you smoked dope. You were a regular at the drop-in center where we talked to Jennie. You told people how to get their shit together, how much human potential they had. Then one day you were found in a coma. You'd been drinking, and the paramedics came and took you to the hospital. And when you woke up, you had no idea who you were and where you came from. You said you had no family. You were a man without a past. And then you finally admitted after about a month in the hospital that you had family back in North Dakota, and they called me." Now it was my turn to be angry. "Don't you remember a goddamn thing?" I was furious at that brilliant brain of his, turned blank by his life.

"That so?" he finally said. He looked lost.

"That is *truly* so." My anger and resentment dissolved. "I'm sorry we let you go so long. That you ended up here. It must have been...I don't know, lonely."

"I do remember some things, faces, sounds. I recall having nothing to hang on to anymore. I remember rolling down a long hill, like the one we tobogganed on in Bismarck. Maybe I dreamt that. I just kept *rolling and rolling*, down and down, faster and faster. People called after me but I was going too fast to stop and see who they were. I remember Land's End."

"Looking for your old apartment? You got pretty close to Land's End Aloft." That was the name he had given to his long-ago apartment on the Great Highway near Ocean Beach.

"That's it, bro. I figured if I could find that old place, I'd be home free. Like old times. But I never got there."

He lit a cigarette, lay back on the grass, and gazed up to the tops of the trees. "I fucked it up?"

the build up is getting frustrating.

I didn't have the heart to answer. I was after bigger things. "So you remembered you had a brother back in Bismarck. Did you remember anything about me? My life back there? My wife? My daughters, Frances and Clare?"

"It's shadowy. You were married. She's gone, yes?"

"She died. Six years ago."

"Suicide?"

Good. Something had moved. Long-term met short-term. "Overdosed on pills."

"Sorry."

"Do you remember anything else about her?"

"Nice lady. What was her name?"

"Jeanne Marie." Jesus, he didn't even remember her name.

"Right. A shame she died."

"Yes it was."

"She'd been depressed for a long time, hadn't she?"

"Yes. Very." That, but not her name. Amazing.

"Overdosed on anti-depressants?" Nick asked. The doctor was in and asking questions. "How'd she get the pills?"

"I don't know. Did she ever talk to you about her addiction?"

"I vaguely remember her asking me for my professional opinion once or twice. How to fight depression. We probably talked about imagining herself in the most beautiful place possible. And hold that image. That's about it. I told that to everyone."

"She found someone who gave her pills. Lots of them." For six years I'd suspected that Nick furnished her with the drugs she used to kill herself. She would never tell me where she found them.

FINALLY!

"Not me," Nick said. "I couldn't prescribe pills. Her death—a goddamn shame. Listen, I'm hungry again. Let's go."

I squeezed his arm so tightly he recoiled. "So you never sent her drugs?" I knew Jeanne Marie hated his late-night phone calls as much as I did, his maudlin self-pity, his mean streak. But I knew she asked him questions about medications, about mental illness, especially when I was working late and she was home alone. She'd laughed when she told me what he told her. There was something about Nick that attracted her.

She often told me she was sick of North Dakota. She often talked about moving to California. I always heard it as a wish rather than a declaration. And we both knew I was lucky to be at a high school that valued four years of Latin. So what if it was in North Dakota? Would I have found a better school in California? I doubted it. But I'd spent a lot of sleepless nights worrying about why she wanted to move there.

I grasped his shoulders and shook him gently. "Nick, are you sure you never sent her drugs?" I wasn't about to let go of it.

"I *think* I'd remember *that*. So *no*! Sorry, I can't help. But I *can* tell you I have an enormous appetite and would like to leave here now. If we could have Chinese delivered here, I'd be happy to stay. I see no food stands. Come on, brother."

"Would you listen to me for once, just once! I think you furnished Jeanne Marie with prescription pills. I can't prove it. You've got to tell me, Nick. I've got to know."

"I told you, no, no, no, and *no*."

"You're lying! You son of a bitch, tell me the truth!" Some of the bronzed people nearby stared at us. "Where did she get the pills if not from you?"

"She can't tell you and neither can I. I don't know."

I raised my hand. It was a threatening gesture, as if I was about to strike him. He held his arm in front of his face. He looked frightened. I stared sheepishly at the street people nearby. I lowered my arm. We sat there and said nothing. I waited for my heart rate to slow down. Easy, mister.

That was it. That was all the answer I'd get. I helped him up. I'd spent this afternoon trying to reconstruct the last days of Doctor Nick to get at the last days of my wife's life.

What was his terrible fear of having family back in North Dakota? I'd assumed it was because he was somehow involved in my wife's death. If he was, he'd totally blanked out on it. He

66

believed his own myth—the knowing good doctor who did no harm. Maybe I was wrong. Maybe it wasn't a myth.

We drove in silence back to the bakery that Bonnie and I had visited that morning. There was still a line out the door. Nick wore the cloak of people in a charity food line—shoulders hunched, head down. He seemed shamed. I needed to reestablish contact.

"Sorry I got so angry back there, Nick. Let's get something to eat."

"Sounds good. More like it."

He recovered fast. "Brother, can you spare a dime?" he chirped at a young man walking past us with his girlfriend. The guy laughed.

"I hear the food here is making customers sick," he said to five college-age women ahead of us. "You might want to let us go first and see what happens when we take the first bite. Your whole lives are ahead of you."

"Don't believe him," I said. "The food is fantastic. Stay where you are." They laughed.

"My brother here is trying to have me institutionalized and only you can save me."

"He *is* institutionalized," I said, regretting it immediately. Nick's face turned red, menacing even.

"Fuck that!" he shouted. The young women turned away from us. Luckily the line ahead had moved and they disappeared inside. We were next. He was not mollified.

"Why did you do that?" he demanded. "'Institutionalized.' You continue to be an asshole."

We just stood there looking at each other. I hoped it would be the lowest point of my visit. We slipped inside and ordered.

Our meal passed in an icy silence. Nick ordered two prosciutto and provolone panini, plus an omelet and vegetables and two chocolate chip cookies. He ate it all. I was hoping that the cathedral had a convenient restroom. He would need one.

"You wearing a senior diaper?" I asked.

"You wearing a senior condom?" he shot back.

"Nick, one, Ben, zero," I admitted. That was enough to melt the ice. We both laughed, he harder than I.

We left the bakery and returned to the van. Nick reminisced about his early love for Haydn's cello concertos. Great, maybe he would be on good behavior tonight. We drove to Market Street, turned and drove until we finally reached Cathedral Hill. Streets were packed with concertgoers. There was no parking near the church. I was wondering how far Nick could walk without collapsing. I saw a spot open up just two blocks away from the church and raced to beat out a BMW coming from the opposite direction.

"Nice maneuver," Nick observed. He had always been an aggressive driver, honking at anyone who might try to take *his* parking place.

I squeezed the van into the space. We trudged the two blocks. It was slow going. I was glad we had left plenty of time to get there. Outside, a line of people was waiting to buy tickets. On the edge of the crowd stood Bonnie and Joyce.

Seeing the two of them standing there—Bonnie smiling, expectant; Joyce tight-lipped, in an erect, show-me posture—I felt a sensation I hadn't experienced since high school. The minute I arrived at the home of Virginia Traxler to take her to the senior prom, I knew it was a mistake. She was the last person I should be going to prom with. I hardly knew her, but I had put off asking anyone, too busy playing baseball and filling out college admission forms. Virginia had been dumped by her date three days before the prom. So the powers that be—the school principal and our homeroom teacher—coached me on how to invite her, how to pick out a corsage, even how to ring her doorbell. And they warned me about Virginia's mother.

So that prom night, I rang the doorbell, holding a corsage chosen by my teacher. Standing *behind* her mother, Virginia looked expectant and teary. Her mother looked me up and down like a policewoman. I was so sexually unsure of myself, I wilted under the side-by-side auras of Virginia's hopeful anticipation and her mother's resolute wrath. The mother saw me as a substitute, a stand-in, a dummy, and a jerk no better than the other guy who had stood up her darling daughter. I said hi to the two of them as the mother grabbed the corsage and pinned it on Virginia.

I asked if I could use the bathroom. The mother left Virginia standing there and led me by the elbow to the bathroom, then grabbed me by my bow tie. "You make one move on my Virginia, and her two brothers will tear you into little pieces." All the while she was talking, she was tightening my bow tie until I started to choke. Then as quickly as she'd grabbed me, she loosened her grip, straightened my tie and smiled sweetly.

Virginia and I had an awful time at the prom. Classmates whispered mean things about us. I never knew why. One guy came after me when I told him to go fuck himself. Classmates pulled us apart.

We left the prom early. I had enough courage to give her a little peck on the cheek at the door. I never had anything to do with her the rest of the school year, and never heard anything about her after graduation. But under my yearbook picture, the editor added a sentence to my profile. "Girls are safe with Sir Ben."

Why I thought about Virginia Traxler at that moment mystified me. Maybe it was the "Sir Ben" in my yearbook profile. Women were safe with me. And they knew it. But my wife had not been safe with me. I had not saved her from herself. And maybe not from Nick either.

"You guys are right on time." That was Joyce. To my surprise she came over and kissed Nick and me on the cheek. I figured Bonnie had scripted Joyce to *not* be mean.

Even Nick looked surprised. "*Muy mutual,*" he said.

Bonnie hugged me. I held her shoulders and kissed her on the cheek. She gave Nick a hug and he squeezed her.

"Thanks for the invitation," I said. "Nick is a Haydn aficionado. I'm educable."

"I'm pleased you wanted to come," said Bonnie

"You guys look reasonably sharp," Joyce said. Nick was in his fleece multicolor jacket and chinos. I was wearing what I had worn that morning for my coffee with Bonnie. I cringed a little. I wished I'd changed. The two of them, of course, were exquisitely dressed, Joyce in a navy jacket, linen top and black slacks, and Bonnie in a white top, red silk jacket and tan skirt.

"How much do we owe you for the tickets?" I asked.

"Thirty-six bucks," Joyce replied. "C'mon, let's go inside and get a seat. Pay me later." We went inside. We made quite a foursome, the two of them and the two of us.

I was just glad for a break from being alone with Nick. Inside, the soaring canopy of the Cathedral of St. Mary of the Assumption hung above us, like an enormous hot-air balloon tethered to earth by four concrete pylons. Triangular latticework graced the surface of the canopy. Two perpendicular rivulets of red and blue stained glass broke through the canopy far above. It felt good, this ethereal place.

On the raised sanctuary floor before the high altar, the chorus and the musicians were finding their seats. Every spot in the center of the fan-shaped nave was occupied, so we found an empty pew at the left edge of the congregation. Bonnie sat next to me, Joyce on her other side, and Nick at the other end. I passed programs along to Bonnie and she gave two of them to Joyce.

Nick fidgeted with his program and made loud sighs. Some people craned their necks to see who was making the racket. He pointed at me. I was glad we were off to the side.

Just then, the conductor strode across the floor of the cathedral. Her magisterial bearing—with a long black skirt down to her ankles and a black velvet jacket—was capped by jet-black-rimmed glasses. Her stride across the nave, high heels clicking, drew applause.

"I wouldn't mind having *her* drop down on me in Stern Grove," said Nick, looking at no one in particular. I ignored him. The maestra bowed, tapped the podium, and the music began. On cue, the choir joined the orchestra.

The cathedral almost shook with the power of the massed voices. *"Now vanish before the holy beams the gloomy dismal shades of dark..."* I shivered.

Next to me, Bonnie was whispering the text—in German, ever so silently. *"Nun schwanden vor dem heiligen Strahle."* I turned to look at her. Her face reddened and she switched to English.

"Now vanish before the holy beams," she whispered. "The first of days appears."

I smiled.

"I taught basic German for years."

Joyce shushed us and leaned forward, as if to better focus. Nick's eyes were shut. His right-hand index finger wagged just below the top of the pew, conducting. When "The Heavens Are Telling the Glory of God" anthem concluded, the whole place erupted in applause.

At intermission we went outside to the cathedral plaza. We looked up at the stars emerging in the twilight. Joyce joked about how good a job God had done millions of years ago. Bonnie spoke in rushed ecstatics about the score. "In the history of choral music I believe there is no greater synergy between score and text than what we're hearing tonight. The soars and swells capture the work of creation and the grandeur of the cosmos. It just takes your breath away."

"Being a nun gave Bonnie culture," said Joyce. "And time. She didn't have to raise kids. I once described Bonnie's lifestyle as 'Her and her none.'"

I laughed hard. Bonnie laughed too.

"You detect a little resentment?" Bonnie asked.

"Of course!" she guffawed. "But it passed. Bonnie took

advantage of the freedom. She loved teaching, and learning. She was a *woman* of the world."

"My favorite riff on the word 'nun' is..." started Nick. I braced myself. "...nun means never had none, never going to get none. Until now, right?"

My instinct was to protect Bonnie. I expected the by-now-familiar Bonnie blush, but she just laughed. "We were not cloistered, don't forget. Any woman who was a nun in this country during the 1970s and 1980s saw a lot, or she wasn't conscious. And Nick, it's not true I never had none. I had a little. I held hands with priests at encounter groups, kissed them at the Grotto at Notre Dame during summer sessions. I skirted the edges of intimacy."

"And now here we are again," Joyce smiled at her friend. "I raised three kids pretty much on my own, both before and after my ex split. But when girl friend here left the convent, well, 'yippee' says it best!"

Nick lit another cigarette. He looked distracted, anxious. "What's happening after the creation?"

"The fall," I replied. The women laughed. Nick didn't.

Turning to Bonnie, I asked, "Do you believe in God?"

"What's the alternative?" she asked me.

"Oy vey," Nick said. "Such a good Jewish response, to answer a question with a question."

Joyce laughed again.

"Agnosticism or atheism," I said.

"The one who defines the terms will win the argument," Bonnie said. "I believe there is something divine about us all, male and female. God and Adam and Eve. The original trinity, the lover and the beloved." I nodded. Nick smiled.

People were moving back inside. We followed the crowd. Rivulets of stained glass above us looked like the fingers of God cracking through the canopy. They reminded me of Michelangelo's magnificent fresco—God's finger reaching down to create Adam.

"Where's the privy?" Nick asked, coughing as he stepped

on his cigarette. I nodded in the general direction and we peeled off from Bonnie and Joyce. Nick was limping, dragging his right foot. We followed the signs and took an elevator to the lower level in the back of the church.

Outside the door, Nick said, "I'll be okay, bro."

"Quiet when you come back, huh?" I tried not to sound too teacherish. He groaned and limped into a stall.

Joyce, Bonnie and I listened as baritone Adam and soprano Eve sang their hearts out at the bliss, rapture and wonderment of being alive together.

We all heard the sound at the same time. I knew it was Nick shuffling across the floor of the cathedral, right in the middle of a heartbreaking passage in Eve's aria. The shoe on his bad leg scraped across the floor like a heavy bag of nails over loose pebbles. People in the center of the church were looking sideways.

The singer playing Eve barely kept her eyes heavenward. I could swear I saw Adam move his lips in a quick curse. Nick was crashing the Eden scene. I wanted to crawl under the pew.

Suddenly, there he was, heading right for the orchestra, shuffling like a child on skates, feet never leaving the floor, listing a little to the opposite side of the leg he was favoring. I started out but there was a good hundred feet between us. He pressed on. The whole church seemed to hold its breath. I went into the middle aisle and—waved. He crossed over to me. By this time the chorus members had stopped looking at their songbooks and were glaring at Nick. The conductor turned her head, peering over her graceful glasses in time to see him half-limping on his good leg, and me dragging him by the arm. Bonnie looked mortified and Joyce buried her head in her hands. I tried to push him into the pew. The orchestra was playing something soft and tender. With arms outstretched for balance, Nick twirled around, stopped, teetered, and then did another pirouette. "Singing has led to dancing," he whispered to us. An usher approached us. Nick hung on to the pew's armrest, glared at those who were glaring at him, made the sign of the cross over them, and sat down. "Mission accomplished," he whispered.

The four of us stood with the audience but waited for everyone else to leave. "My god, that is the most beautiful music," Joyce said. "You'll stop up?" She did not say "Please."

Bonnie said it. "Yes, please, come over. I baked a cake." She took my arm. "We insist."

"But *you*," Joyce pointed to Nick, "behave!" We all knew what she meant.

I wondered about Nick's strength after two nights out and the stress of this afternoon's scene in Golden Gate Park. And that shuffling gait was alarming. I hadn't paid much attention to it until now, as we walked down the street toward the van.

The departing audience members had given us a wide right-of-way. Some musicians approached, carrying their instrument cases. I pushed Nick to the other side of the street. I heard one of them say, "That's him." Seeing them hauling cellos and horns and woodwinds, Nick yelled out. "Thanks, gentle musicians! We have shed the heavy wraps of earthly existence—except for the need to shit." They pretended they didn't hear him.

He pushed my steering arm away. He was no longer limping. Had it been an act? Nick seemed to gather strength with every step—would tonight be a repeat of last night's exhibition? At that moment I felt desperate for my brother to be someone else—a fun guy to hang out with. But he was Nick and that was that.

Only this morning I thought how great it would be if these two women had a relationship with Nick after I went back to Bismarck. Dumb, dumb, dumb. It was way too late to mainstream my brother.

"We have a surprise!" Joyce announced as Nick and I stepped off the elevator at her condo. I had faith that her surprise would appeal to him and wouldn't aggravate his condition. We walked into the living room and there it was: a big bass fiddle. Nick eyed it ravenously.

Joyce handed him the bow. "You were telling us, Nick, how you were jamming up and down the coast back in the day. This fiddle belongs to my son's friend, Daunte." Nick's eyes popped. A smile sprinted across his face. He ran his hand up and down the wood.

"Nice," he whispered. Joyce went to the Baby Grand. She started slowly, playing a variation on "Lullaby of Birdland." Nick eased himself onto a stool and started plucking the strings. He looked transformed. Maybe he wouldn't need beer tonight.

Bonnie disappeared into the kitchen. Nick's tempo pulled alongside Joyce's fast-fingered syncopation. Shutting his eyes, he hit his stride.

I stood next to Joyce. "You're *very* good."

"I was a music major in college." She had the piano-bar gift of gab while playing. "Just another music major making it as a real estate agent, which allows me to indulge my major musical loves. My very own Steinway. Used, of course. Business has been good."

I nodded. "I bet you've had to be twice as good as anyone else for a long time."

"I did indeed. Plus one or two lucky breaks. Eighty-hour weeks, weekdays and weekends."

I found it remarkable that a Black realtor was making it in this city. "Anybody try to tell you that you should be selling real estate in Oakland, not San Francisco?" She smiled at the question.

"I got my start there. But I had a friend named Sister Bonnie and she had a daddy who ran an investment company, and I handled the sale of his place in North Beach. Word spread. And I got real good at what I did."

She was doing riffs toward the end of "Lullaby of Birdland," and then she and Nick ended with a sweet, breathtaking glissando of keys and strings. I clapped. Nick bowed and Joyce smiled. Bonnie brought in a tray of glasses.

"Coke, juice, mineral water and cake all around," she announced.

"No beer?" Nick asked. "Two beers, please."

"No beer, Nick," she said, friendlier than I would have.

"How can I stroke this fiddle without a real beer?"

"Suck it up, Nick," Joyce said.

Nick chug-a-lugged a Coke.

"'The Nearness of You,'" Joyce announced. "Dancing music." She started off solo, but Nick caught up after a little fussing with a string. Bonnie walked up to me and took my hand. I slipped an arm around her waist and we slow-danced. Joyce made "The Nearness of You" shimmer, notes glimmering in the silence that followed. She got up and turned on a stereo.

Nick hugged the fiddle as he gulped down another Coke. Joyce took his glass, set it down and got him dancing. He was dragging his foot again. Joyce put her arms around his neck. I thought that was a little risky but I realized it was actually a neck grip so she could apply pressure if he pushed against her too tightly. He just kind of swayed back and forth with her. He had a wild, panicky look in his eyes.

"The bathroom calls," Nick announced. "Carry on without me." He charged out of the room. When he was gone, I said I'd clean up after him. Joyce said not to worry about it and returned to the piano seat.

Bonnie and I stood on either side of her. Joyce started riffing on "Climb Every Mountain." She looked at Bonnie. "Dedicated to Bonnie, just six months out of the convent. Onward and upward!"

Then she started improvising on melodies from *Porgy and Bess*. I'd never heard the songs spun the way she did: "A Woman is a Sometime Thing." "Summertime." "I Got Plenty o' Nuttin'." Bonnie and I hung on the side of the piano. It was just the three of us.

Nick had been gone about twenty minutes. I thought of him once but I knew he spent a lot of time in the bathroom so I wasn't worried at first. Then I thought I'd better check.

I rapped on the bathroom door. "Nick, you okay?" I hadn't even tried the handle. I knew it was locked.

"Nick, what's going on?" Silence.

I yelled, "Say something—or open the door!" Not a sound. Bonnie and Joyce were right behind me.

"Nick, open the door or we're coming in," Joyce commanded. I heard something move.

"Nick, what the hell's going on in there?" The movement stopped. "Nick?" Then I heard him guzzling liquid.

"Could he have found booze?" I asked Joyce.

She shook her head. "There's no beer in the frig, real or non-alcoholic, and wine and liquor are locked in a concealed cabinet. Nothing."

I was frantic. Despite her reassurance, booze was the only thing I could think of. "If he's drinking, his blood sugar will drop like a stone! Nick, open the goddamn door!"

"We could force the door," said Bonnie. She looked at Joyce, who clearly did not like the idea.

"Nick, we're about to break down the door. And then I'm going to break your goddamn arm! Open up."

"Who's calling?" Finally, some back talk.

"Nick, if you don't open this door..." It was Joyce, her voice powerful, and her threat credible. "I'll call the cops and tell them you crashed my condo. You'll spend the next three days crawling the walls of some miserable drunk tank. They couldn't give a shit that you are Doctor Nick or that you're diabetic. You may never wake up again! You hear me?" She was screaming now.

Suddenly she looked at me. "Oh my god, I know what he found. There were three bottles of this boutique Belgian beer, a year old at least, in the back of the pantry. Somebody gave them to me. I totally forgot."

"What the hell is going on when I can't drink a beer or two in peace? My Midwestern brother continues to labor under the lies and distortions of the Minnesota total abstinence establishment." He was blurring all his words. "Here on the coast, we know anyone can drink, if they know their limits. The Rand Corporation study proved it."

We heard him smash a bottle, probably against the bathtub, and then another one, and then a third. He had finished all three. We could hear cabinets slamming.

"Easy on the furniture in there! I have no drugs, no cough syrup, nothing," Joyce said.

"Nick, why don't you come out and we can party?" It was Bonnie. "We sundowners."

"Say more. I like that idea. My brother, the tight-ass from No-Dak, won't approve, but we sundowners can party away the night in revelry."

Joyce shook her head. Bonnie nestled in close to the door and spoke in a low, warm voice. "I want to talk about how you started the night revels program, Nick. How did you pull the sundowning rabbit out of your clinical psychology hat? How does it all fit together? Maybe I can help."

Nick unlocked the door but opened it only a couple of inches. "Say more, Bonnie."

Bonnie clung to her side of the door, and Nick slowly pushed it open. There he stood, a grotesque figure with lethargic eyes. He had his clothes on, thank god. Broken glass glistened on the tiled floor.

"Come on, Nick. Back to the living room." Bonnie reached out to him. He stepped over the glass, took her hand, and, like a small child, walked past Joyce, whom he saluted, and me, to whom he shot a victorious grin. The son of a bitch. He must have found the beer and planned this last night.

Joyce came close to me. "I am a generous person," she whispered. "I have wide limits, but Doctor Nick has surpassed them. Now Bonnie's going to mother him to death. Would you please get his ass back to Sunnyslope or over to San Francisco

General, whatever, before he pukes and passes out on my living room rug. Your brother is more than demented, he is fucking dangerous. Oh my god, look at all the glass! How did he escape getting gashed?"

I was hoping she wasn't as furious as she sounded. Nick needed orange juice, something to get him stable before he keeled over and really complicated things. Joyce was way ahead of me. She had ducked into the kitchen and was returning with a glass of juice, which she gave to Bonnie.

Nick teetered as he stepped on to a living room throw rug. He backed up toward the sliding door leading out to the balcony.

Bonnie held up the orange juice glass in front of Nick's face.

"Screwdriver?" Nick said.

"Vodka three to one," Bonnie answered. He shot her an unbelieving glance. "Drink it all down, Nick." Nick smelled it and held it to his lips.

He chugged it down. He snarled. "You lied."

Undaunted, Bonnie gently tugged his sleeve. "So tell us about humanistic psychology." She walked him back to the sofa, helped him onto it and sat facing him on an ottoman. Evidently she thought he would come down gradually and sink into sleep on the floor. I looked at Joyce, who had a telephone in her hand, ready to call the paramedics.

"What led you to the revels of the night?" Bonnie started to scribble on the back of a magazine. "I need your help if you want me to help."

Nick stood up, reached for a pack of cigarettes and turned to the balcony door. Joyce beat him to the door. He would have to push her through the glass to get out to the balcony. Joyce held up her arms like she was summoning some martial art, ready to toss him to the floor. Nick turned to face Bonnie and me, holding an unlit cigarette in his mouth, and started pacing.

Suddenly, as if sober, he began: "First, let me say I'm a humanistic psychologist. That movement is our only hope against the night, against annihilation, against the naysayers of Christianity. The blessed light of the holy trinity of Carl, Abraham and Rollo has shone upon us! I arise to sing and dance and beat back the forces of darkness, the doomsayers who have inserted sin into our very bloodstreams so that we cannot breathe without commingling the enzymes of our humane-ness with the Christian toxins of sinful, fallen humanity."

He lurched toward us. I stepped forward, but he waved me away. Bonnie motioned for me to sit beside her on the ottoman. That seemed like a good idea. Don't threaten him.

I mouthed "nine one one" to Joyce. She left the room.

"Humanistic psychology is called the third wave of twentieth century psychology. You may ask what are the first two?" Nick blinked. He was sweating heavily.

"I don't know, but you are the fourth wave," Joyce yelled from the study. He stood there slack-jawed, flushed, his whole body sagging and weaving. The orange juice was not enough."

"Who are those first two waves?' Bonnie insisted.

"The first wave was behaviorism: B.F. Skinner and his merry band of positivists and empiricists. He pursued the answer to the question, how are we conditioned to behave in certain ways? He explored the role of positive rewards."

He burped and continued. "Other psychologists got lumped together with him: Ivan Pavlov and the conditioned reflex."

Bonnie asked him about the man who taught dogs how to feel helpless.

"Martin Seligman. You isolate the subject and then make sure the dog doesn't know what's coming next. A state of pure passivity."

"Woof, woof!" barked Joyce, returning to the room and holding her hands up like a helpless dog. Nick glared at her. I heard the faint sound of a siren.

Nick grew more agitated. He roamed unsteadily around the room and kept talking. "And do you not think that Nick's recipe for ending sundowning in our time borrows heavily from Skinner? You will not fear the future night if you learn to embrace it. Positive rewards—recognition, self-worth, empathy, all created by the placebos of common, meaningful rituals of the night, food and drink, dancing, touch, stories. No more of this 'failed lives' bullshit! Party on, elders!

"Of course Skinner's findings were subject to all kinds of misuse. Those in power owe a great deal to behaviorism," Nick growled. "Keep your people awash in rewards: food, sex, diversions.

"Wave two," demanded Joyce.

"Psychoanalysis. Freud, Jung, Erikson, Fromm. Consciousness is merely the paltry iceberg cap visible above the unconscious mass below. We go back under analysis to our unconscious drives, exploring the vast continuum between infancy and adulthood."

His face darkened. "Of course it was the goddamn psychiatrists who made the most money on this mother lode. People remain in therapy for years. Or they get the quick fix from doctors prescribing pills, endorsing pills and making millions off pills. I say millions!"

Joyce held up three fingers and waved her hand impatiently. Nick shouted, "Enter humanistic psychology, the third wave. Ta da! It sprang to life in the nineteen fifties through the work of Rollo May, Carl Rogers and Abraham Maslow, among others. Humanistic psychology digs down into what it means to be human. How do we gain fulfillment, self-worth, and autonomy? How do we become human? Forget the unconscious. How do we experience consciousness?" His gaze was becoming unfocused. His hands shook. He crushed the cigarette.

"Maslow unveiled the hierarchy of needs, leading to self-actualization. Carl Rogers gave us client-centered therapy. From these beginnings came encounter groups, Gestalt therapy, and the whole human potential movement."

His face turned ashen, his eyes upward. He seemed to summon energy for one last ride on the waves of history. "From all these formative influences came the revels of the night! From them came—me!"

Nick slouched. He started to tip over. Bonnie sprang to

his side and held on to him. I took his other arm and we laid him on the couch. "Diabetic shock," I yelled. The phone was ringing; we could see the flashing lights of an ambulance on the street outside. It took the paramedics less than a minute to get up to Joyce's apartment. They rolled him onto a stretcher. I said I was his brother and I'd be coming with him.

Joyce asked which hospital they would take him to. It was going to be Saint Francis Memorial Hospital. "We'll meet you there," she said. Bonnie nodded.

I crouched into a small space in the back of the ambulance. The paramedics hooked Nick up to oxygen and an intravenous feed. It was touch and go, I was sure.

Why had I made so light of the dangers? What was I doing treating this as a date night? I had a sick man—dying man, really—on a simple day pass. I had given myself an easy task—keep a few simple rules, avoid alcohol, beware of entanglement. I had taken him out for fun tonight, but he had a different idea of fun and he was going to have it his way. Now he was near death.

In the emergency room, the ER team worked fast to stabilize Nick. I told a nurse that he had been a patient in San Francisco General a year ago and his records were there. I was sent out to the family waiting room. Bonnie and Joyce were already there and hugged me. They both looked pale.

"We have witnessed a marvel tonight, oh yes," Joyce began as soon as I sat down. "I've been around drunks, but none of them can equal your brother."

"My brother is the fourth wave, as you said back at your place. He's waiting, just waiting, to swamp you."

"I. Am. Swamped." She punctuated each pause.

Bonnie stood up, took my hand and held it. Her eyes were bloodshot and swollen.

I spoke quietly. "You two ought to go home. Forty-eight hours ago you didn't know me from...."

"...Adam," Joyce inserted. "And now we've all been thrown out of Eden."

The ER medic came out through swinging doors. He had thick bushy hair, a cautious smile, and a smooth, ageless face. "Nick's brother, right?" I nodded and we shook hands. "I'm Dr. Sharma. We've got him stabilized. His vitals are okay for now, but your brother needs a work-up tomorrow, a look at the medications he's using, that kind of thing. I suggest you get some sleep and come back tomorrow morning. By then we'll have him in another unit. Are you close by?"

"Ben, my place is five minutes away. Stay with us tonight. I'll give the nurse my number," said Joyce. Dr. Sharma nodded to her.

I said we'd stick around awhile. I called Consuela and José, and told them Nick was in the hospital overnight but should be out tomorrow. Consuela asked questions, lots of questions, one spilling into the next. I could feel the accusation in her voice—I didn't blame her, but I kept my answers to a minimum.

The three of us waited for an hour. I wasn't quite ready to leave Nick alone. I thought of what Bonnie had said early this morning—our match-up in Stern Grove was a lark. But this was no lark. This was an abysmal mismatch of people, Nick and me, and the two of them. We didn't belong in the same story. And yet here we were, because of a serendipitous impulse encounter.

"I'm sorry, Ben, about the beer." Joyce looked ready to cry. "I never even remembered I had them."

"I should never have got him started on psychology," Bonnie said in a whisper. "We wasted time. I thought he'd sober up."

I started to laugh. "You two! What did he call us? 'My anxiety-ridden brother and his west coast girlfriends.'" They started laughing and we all broke down and whooped.

Dr. Sharma pushed through the door and looked puzzled over our merriment. "Your brother could really use a liver transplant," he said matter-of-factly, looking up from a stash of papers inside a plastic folder. "We had his file sent from San Francisco General. Cirrhosis has eaten away more at his liver. As his brother, you might be the ideal donor."

My breath caught in my throat.

"Unfortunately, his general physical condition is too compromised so I would recommend against it. His other organs, brain, heart...damaged. He's lived hard, I'd guess." He looked suggestively at the three of us and for a moment I felt guilty, as if I'd been out there hard-living with him.

"How long will he live?" I asked.

"He could go anytime. I'd guess heart attack. He's probably had small ones in the past from the way his heart sounds. I understand he's in a board and care situation. He's not hospice material yet. He should be okay where he's living. They know how to deal with him."

"Better than I do," I said.

"I'd like to have him talk to a therapist here. I see he was a clinical psychologist. You know how medical doctors and psychologists have it in for each other."

I grimaced and nodded.

"When he left the hospital a year ago after being picked up in the park, their records show they sent him home with lots of pills. Don't worry. I won't load him up with more." He smiled a big enigmatic smile.

"Can I talk to him for a minute?"

"Of course. You'll be doing the talking."

Joyce patted my shoulders. I went into the ER unit. Nick was hooked up to a heart monitor and an IV feed. His eyelids were closed.

"Nick, it's Ben. How're you feeling?" He managed a small wave of a finger, the same motion he used in conducting music in the church pew and on the grassy hillside. He wasn't as agitated as I expected.

He whispered something inaudible. I said, "I'm guessing you said, 'Get me the hell out of here, we are wasting precious hours.' Not to worry. Hello from Bonnie and Joyce."

In the quiet of his room, punctuated only by the clicking, blinking monitors of heart rate, blood pressure and oxygen levels, I thought of us as an eight-year-old and eleven-year-old crawling over the sheets on our twin beds, yelling, "You drive, I'll sleep." We were always on our way to San Francisco, because we thought we could see it out the bedroom window. Now, here we were.

And suddenly I felt lonelier than I'd ever felt, even lonelier than when Jeanne Marie died. I admitted to myself that I didn't want to be alone with him. I'd used Joyce and Bonnie to keep that from happening except for a couple of hours here and there. The two of them had relieved the ache I felt alone with Nick.

I had started off yesterday in control, or so I thought—don't let him touch alcohol, make sure he takes his pills, ask gently about Jeanne Marie, try to reconstruct his descent, and get him back to Sunnyslope in one piece. Then we met Joyce and Bonnie.

I kissed Nick's forehead and walked out into the hallway. When I got to the waiting room I half expected it to be empty. But Bonnie and Joyce hadn't moved. I wanted to tell them right there that I'd be out of their lives the next morning.

For some reason, I didn't.

When we returned to Joyce's condo after two hours at Saint Francis Memorial, we each reverted to type.

"It's one in the morning and I know where I'm sleeping," Joyce announced, arms on hips. "You two figure out who gets the bedroom and who gets the study." She was pulling towels and bedding for the sofa bed out of a hall closet.

"Why don't you take the other bedroom? You must be exhausted," said Bonnie.

"I like sofa beds. Really. You take the bedroom. If the hospital calls, I won't disturb you."

"Nick will be fine, don't worry," she said.

"Yes, he'll be fine but I have the screaming meemies!" Joyce's voice was three registers high. She banged the linen closet door shut, and threw me the sheets and blankets.

"Goodnight, Bonnie, goodnight, Ben, and goodnight Nick!"

Bonnie spoke reassuringly. "Sleep well." She kissed my cheek, slipped into the bedroom and shut the door.

I slept very lightly. Bonnie knocked at about seven the next morning. I was awake. I had been looking around the room at the photos of Joyce and her three children. A male figure appeared in a couple of early photos, but as the kids grew, he disappeared.

"Morning, Ben."

I sat up on the bed, put my feet on the floor, and got up and stretched. "Morning, Bonnie. Sleep okay?"

"Yes. You?"

"Okay." She stood about five feet away, pushing her hair back from her face. "Come and have breakfast before we go. Joyce fixed eggs and bacon."

"I need a shower. Be right with you. Then I'll be on my way."

"We're coming, too. See you in the kitchen." She shut the door behind her.

Joyce was wearing a chef's white apron. "Eggs over easy and bacon from the farmers market. Coffee's there. Mugs are in the cupboard."

"Nobody called," Bonnie said. "That's good news, I think."

"I can hear him pounding the desk of some poor nurse," I said after a first swallow of coffee. "'I'm Doctor Nick. I want to talk to the medical director of this place. Dr. Sharma's too stingy with the Xanax.'" They both laughed.

I laid out a scenario. "First I get the medical report, second,

I face the music with Consuela and José. For all I know, I'll be
picked apart by San Mateo County social workers."

Last night's "Let's say goodbye" moment at the hospital
between them and me had fizzled. This, however, was a good
time to say goodbye. All I wanted to do was untangle the web I
had woven with these women. Strangers, really.

No one was talking. We sat looking at each other. I was still
eating. I think the incongruity of the three of us being together
just smacked us all at the same time.

Joyce started to say something the same moment I did.
"No, you first," she said.

"Well, I've been thinking."

She interrupted. "How could you be such an asshole as
to have not contacted your brother in six years? I know about
your Alcoholics Anonymous program. I know you can't save
him from himself. But isn't there such a thing as an interven-
tion? Did you really ever try to get him help?"

The questions were evidently rhetorical because she went
right on. "That's first on my agenda. The only person we all
know much about is Nick. Maybe it should stay that way. Ben
doesn't like intruders, people who ask questions." Joyce shoved
her hands down into her bathrobe pockets. "I sense you want
us out of your life. We are, after all, complete strangers." She
leaned against the kitchen counter and smiled to herself. "And
your brother needs you. All of you."

There it was—hit the road, Jack. Bonnie held up a hand
that said *stop*. "I just told Ben we were coming with him to the
hospital."

Joyce folded her arms. "Why?"

Bonnie shot back, "He drank your beer, you should be
there to make sure he's out of trouble."

"I didn't give him beer!" Joyce said, her voice flashing irri-
tation. "He found it, goddamnit!"

"All right, all right, enough about beer." Bonnie backed
off. "I told Ben yesterday that our encounter in Stern Grove
was the prelude to a lark. And I meant it."

"Some lark," said Joyce.

"Nick may *die*." Bonnie emphasized the obvious. "We should see it through. If Ben will let us."

I was still smarting over Joyce's rant about twelve-step programs and my abandoning Nick. "If you will allow me to make one thing clear. My brother fantasizes everything: prowess with women, love affairs, nighttime revels. All bullshit. He fantasizes. He hallucinates. And that's why...."

Bonnie held up her hand. "I think we don't know *how much* is true of what people say about themselves. Maybe Nick does do wonderful things with the men and women at Elder Town. Maybe he did wonderful things as a psychologist. *Maybe*." Again, the obvious.

It was time for a dose of reality therapy.

"When I started teaching Latin at twenty-four, I had my hands full. I was a new husband and our first child was on the way. The phone calls from the coast started out on Friday and Saturday nights, eight o'clock. Over the years, later and later, until eleven was the standard hour to hear from Nick. He was always totally blitzed. He..."

"What did your wife think about Nick?" asked Joyce.

"My wife was understanding at first, but gradually lost patience with him. She had a love-hate thing with Nick. She identified with him. To me, he became a disconnected babbling voice on the phone."

"What did he talk about?" asked Bonnie.

"'Hello. Life is sweet here. What are you doing in that dump? Brother, I am here in Half Moon Bay. What the hell is going on in Bismarck, No Dak? I am a major player in transforming the lives of lovely *frauleins* at Land's End Aloft. Do you hear me? *Transformativo!*'"

I could remember his nocturnal patter verbatim. I told them how he would cry. He'd sob for what seemed like hours, followed by the usual funk, the fury when I said to him, "You sound high or drunk or both." He was enraged that I could link his state of ecstasy to being a flat-out drunk. My opinion only proved to him the staggering gap between Midwestern and coastal sensibilities.

Joyce was listening closely, but I couldn't read her. Bonnie's eyes oozed empathy.

"Then he'd call on Sundays or on a week night, sober, reasonable, engaged. Jeanne Marie and I bounced between hating him and forgiving him. I joined a local Alanon group. I know, that's the rap on the Midwest when we're at our wit's end. We're good at it. I learned I didn't have to put up with his rant. I started hanging up on him. Eventually, I dropped him from my life. 'Let go, let God,' they say. I let go. I called him, said goodbye, told him not to call until he sobered up. I got caller ID."

"He is your freaking flesh and blood!" Joyce railed. "You're supposed to stay in touch, you don't let him go off a cliff! Of course he ends up on the street saying he has no family!"

"You don't know what the hell you're talking about!" I couldn't believe she didn't understand. I walked over to the kitchen door. "I think I should be thanking you both and making my way back to the hospital."

Joyce stepped in front of me and planted her hands on my shoulders. "Don't go. Not yet. I'm sorry. We'll see this through for another twenty-four hours." She turned, walked into the living room and opened the balcony door. Bonnie took me by the arm and we trailed after her. I slouched in an armchair facing them on the sofa. We all took some deep breaths. It was a sunny morning and the air felt soothing.

"This is the first time in many years I've talked to another human being about my brother and me. I resent anyone's judgment on my behavior. Suggestions, yes. Condemnation, no. Here's my point. It's called family fatigue. Lots of people drift away from the fringe members of their families. The alcoholic, the can't-keep-a-job, the depressive off his meds, the neurotic, the divorced and drifting self-pitier. We get tired of giving and not getting anything back." I emphasized every word of that last sentence. "We jettison the miserable bastards," I added in almost a whisper.

"I hear you," said Joyce. "I really do get it why you'd do what you did."

"I buried myself in my work. I channeled my energy into teaching. At age fifty-five I didn't want to have to stew over the welfare of my only sibling. I had my own family to think about."

"And the deteriorating sibling refused to get help," said Bonnie.

"I knew the call would come some day. It did." I shrugged and shook my head. "A year later I showed up. I'm not proud of that."

Bonnie bit her fingernails. Joyce poured more coffee. "In my family," said Joyce, "my siblings all lived within twenty miles of each other. No way we could escape each other for six days, much less six months. No way could we drop a sibling. In your face twenty-four/seven."

"My brothers are glued to me," Bonnie said. "I guess I'm lucky,"

"You are. And then, there's my wife."

"Tell us," said Joyce. I started out toward the balcony. It made talking easier.

"I'll tell you the short version. Jeanne Marie and I met in college, dated off and on. I went on to get a degree in classics, she went into nursing. We married when I started teaching. We were a typical couple raising kids in Bismarck. We were great side-by-side, we were good parents. Two daughters. We had a few serious bumps along the way."

"Meaning...?" asked Joyce.

"She suffered from depression."

"When did she die?" asked Bonnie.

"Six years ago, 1991."

"Tell us," Joyce said again.

"Suicide. Pills."

Bonnie asked, "Did you ask him for help with her depression?"

"I believe Nick somehow screwed with her mind. She confided in him. Maybe he even got her drugs, painkillers. I never knew for sure." I hadn't ever said this aloud. Not even to my daughters.

"Did you not *want* to know?" asked Bonnie. "You and your wife never saw a therapist for her depression? You never got to the bottom of it?"

"I went with her once to see her therapist. Jeanne Marie glared at me when I brought up his name. 'Leave Nick out of this. He's got nothing to do with my illness. He's a sick man himself. Why would I want anything from him?' The therapist didn't push her when she blurted out, 'Why would I want anything from him?' And neither did I. We should have pushed her."

I leaned my head against the back of the chair. "That was the reason why I came here Saturday—to find out, did he or didn't he? Yesterday, in Golden Gate Park, I asked Nick if he ever gave drugs to Jeanne Marie."

"And?" Joyce and Bonnie said it at the same time.

"He only said, '"I'd remember *that*. So *no!*' I almost hit him, I was so angry. I don't believe him."

Joyce sat on the edge of her cushion, leaning toward me. "Okay. Right now you've got a brother who needs your help. And whatever else Nick is now, he's been clean for a year, until last night. You may never know whether he supplied her with painkillers. Maybe you just spend time with him in his last days. Maybe you don't hide in your teaching job. You stay awhile. You give up the search for answers about Nick and your wife. Right now, he's just your brother, your sick brother. And maybe, just maybe, you let us help."

I maneuvered my way out to the balcony. I wanted to be anywhere else. I leaned against the railing and looked over the city. I was shaking. I turned to face them.

Bonnie was standing there, leaning against the balcony

door. "Remember the *Aeneid*? 'Even here you can find tears for the suffering of others. Misfortune melts the heart.' She came closer to me. "I think I can help. Our family has a foundation."

Puzzled, I looked at her and waited. She appeared to be thinking about what she had said. No more lark. Time for an agenda.

It felt good, foreign, but good, this yielding to entanglement.

"We give away hundreds of thousands of dollars, both in the U.S. and the Americas. We're a family foundation." Bonnie was all business as she and I returned inside and sat down with Joyce.

"A *Catholic* family foundation," Joyce said.

"*All* Catholic, *all* the time," laughed Bonnie. We give to Catholic causes and organizations, and we fund efforts that help Catholics, for instance, projects for people in South America."

"So a lapsed Catholic from San Mateo espousing free love and atheism—what am I missing here?" Again, puzzled.

Bonnie ignored me. "My father and my brothers all insist that I take over as president. I'm sure there are messages all over my voicemail today. Every day it's the same: 'Bonnie, why are you being so damned obstinate?' I won't say yes and I won't say no, but I'm thinking I'll say yes."

"Tell him about Uncle Matthew," Joyce urged Bonnie.

Bonnie laughed. "You don't need to know....well, it *is* scandalous. The board insists we do a full investigation into the faith of the people we fund. Are they *devout* Catholics?"

"The bar is high," said Joyce.

"Way high over Nick," I said. "He can't even *play* devout."

"If we find out that a prospective grantee ever once spoke in favor of contraception or against a bishop or was part of a church reform movement, that's it. Uncle Matthew sees himself as the chief investigator of faith and morals. He reports back to the board. And the board members compete about who can be the most rigorous in deciding who gets grants. They recently kept a poor church in Texas waiting because the pastor's last name was Hefner and they were sure he was related to Playboy Hugh. We spent three thousand dollars on a family-tree check."

Why had she even brought up this bastion of Catholicism, I thought. "And your parents. What do they think?"

"They shake their heads and stay out of it. But they want me to take it over and restore some sanity. And maybe my first project is a research grant—the night revels at Elder Town."

"Uncle Matthew would run Nick through with a Knights of Columbus sword after two minutes with him!"

"Oh, well. I have my ways of dealing with him," Bonnie said slyly.

She took my hands in hers. "I have to leave town on foundation business in two weeks. But I think I could get a proposal together in a week or so. We have to find the right hook, something like restoring a healthy nostalgia in seniors' lives, reconnecting them with their childhood faith, optimism."

It was preposterous, this scheme, and there was an easy way to deflate it. "Let me take you both to Elder Town. We will go to Nick's house of mirrors together."

"Good! Let's do that," said Bonnie. "Then I can report to Uncle Matthew that I did a preliminary site visit."

"Think positive, Ben," Joyce said. "Nick was using serious drugs when your wife died. This year he's been off drugs until last night. He's been sober at Elder Town. He may not be as delusional as you fear."

"I really think his program is on to something important," said Bonnie. "It's too promising to let die with him, is what I mean."

They might be right. I was about to bet on it. I retreated to the study and called the secretary at Bismarck High School. The principal came to the phone.

"Gone west, right?" she asked without a hello.

"Yeah, right. You remembered. Um...Need time."

"How much?"

"Two weeks."

Dead air followed. "We'll arrange for a sub." She hung up, clearly not happy.

Just six years ago, Bismarck High School, this principal, the faculty and all the students had rallied around me when I lost Jeanne Marie. I knew there was no other profession in which colleagues would offer more unrelenting support. I knew there was no other profession where great hordes of young people would have propped up someone in my situation with hugs, tears and letters. A brother didn't seem to warrant the same response.

I notified the airline that I had to postpone my return to Bismarck and I left the date open. That bothered me more than anything. I wanted Nick and me resolved, case closed, and I wanted to know when.

We took separate cars to the hospital. Nick had been moved from intensive care to a double room. The first thing I noticed was that the second bed was empty. Thank god.

Nick was pacing, hands behind his back. He looked frisky. He'd recovered fast. "Hey, Nick," I greeted him, but hung back as Bonnie and Joyce hugged him. A nurse came in and said his vital signs were all pretty good. "But not as good as his double-entendres," she half-grinned. "Dr. Sharma will be in shortly."

Nick's hospital gown was poorly tied, leaving his backside exposed. He let me tie it while he complained nonstop. I put my hand on his shoulder, my way of hugging.

"Hah, you three thought you could ditch ol' Nick. We'll have none of that bullshit. I'm on the mend. Sharma—who is very stingy with the painkillers by the way—says I'm making remarkable progress. He and I are like *that*." He held up his right hand, and with his index and middle finger joined, fleshed out their simpatico.

"We're going out to Elder Town," I said. I tried to toss out the next sentence in as light a tone as I could find. "We're going to talk to your friends about the sundown program."

"What?"

"Bonnie and Joyce found your ideas about the nighttime revels really interesting." My words were neutral enough. It was my tone of skepticism that must have unleashed his inner warrior.

"Ladies." He cut me off. He was furious. "Go with this man and give me a full report. The lovely Andrea will be my witness for every claim I have made about the sundown program. Goddamnit, I..."

Joyce yelled, "Time out! Fine, we will leave no stone unturned to get at the truth."

Nick bellowed, "My brother here will leave no turn unstoned. He throws rocks at every accomplishment of mine, especially those about which he doesn't know shit from Shinola! He is determined to make me out as a fraud and that pains the hell out of me. He is projecting his own failures, his own neurosis onto me."

Dr. Sharma entered the room, his eyes popping out at the tumult. "Can I help?" he asked quietly.

"Beyond your skill set," said Nick without missing a beat. "Brother here needs psychological counseling."

I could sense the old feelings ramping up again, rage at the sharpened paranoia he kept in his quiver until he shot at whatever threat happened to be advancing. I hated him.

"Nick, I want you to lie down on your bed. I want you to take deep breaths," said Sharma. *"Now!"* Nick complied without hesitation. Sharma had his number.

"You may have earned another day here, and an earlier death with that kind of behavior. You are not a healthy man and I suggest you calm down." Sharma's face was inches from Nick's.

"As one doctor to another," Nick began. "I accept your assessment of my situation."

Sharma smiled. "Good. I invite Ben and...."

"I'm Joyce."

"And I'm Bonnie."

"I suspect, Doctor, they've succumbed to my brother's outrageous ideas about chemical dependency," said Nick.

Sharma held out both hands for a time out. "Okay, Ben. Let's plan on meeting later today. Nick wants you here when I have all the reports back."

"It's Doctor Nick, Doctor," Nick interrupted.

"We can huddle with Doctor Nick about where we go from here."

Sharma walked to the door, turned and sighed. "I'm an ER doc and your brother is an inpatient. But I was asked—well, I volunteered—to be his physician because...well, let's just say there was no competition." He smiled at Nick, who curiously enough looked flattered.

Nick grinned. "Notice: I need special treatment, the guys trained in trauma!" Sharma shrugged and left the room.

When I stepped toward him to say goodbye, Nick brushed my shoulder with a fist. "Watch him," he ordered Bonnie and Joyce. I managed to grab his fist and squeeze his arm.

Once outside and back in the van I pounded the dashboard. "He is cah-razy! What foundation would give my brother a dime?"

"A certain cah-razy Catholic foundation, led by me," answered Bonnie coyly. We left their car in the ramp and were soon hurtling along Highway 101.

this really does not seem like a priority

We pulled up to a modern one-story faux brick building with a cheerily lettered sign attached to the stonework above the front door. "Elder Town Day Activity Center." The building occupied part of a commercial block right in the center of San Mateo. A sign in the window of a small drug store on the corner announced that Corner Drug was going out of business.

Across the street, a brand new CVS was just opening its doors in line with a Wells Fargo bank, pizza parlor and UPS store.

Other than the sign, Elder Town fit right in with its neighbors, in contrast to simple, homey Sunnyslope up the hill where Nick lived. Elder Town's clients were the elderly and its business was keeping them occupied. I could not imagine Nick getting away with anything innovative in this place. I could not imagine him spending time here, with bridge games, bingo sessions, museum visits, Christmas cookies, and jumbo TV screens.

Replaced with nighttime revels? No way. And who was this "lovely Andrea?" Probably some twenty-something social work grad on her first job. She wouldn't know what to do when Doctor Nick crushed her in a slow dance as a Frank Sinatra CD belted out for the billionth time that he had left his heart in San Francisco.

My own jitters about aging had gradually eaten away at my calm, day-at-a-time demeanor. I hadn't given it much thought in my fifties, except for Jeanne Marie's continuing depression and my adult children's school debts. Now in my sixties, with Jeanne Marie gone and the kids doing their fiscal part, I was in the vanguard of a booming population for whom a burgeoning number of strategies tried to make getting old more palatable, even more pleasant.

Any new fad designed to spiff up old age made me cranky. A typical die-hard Midwest attitude. Elder Town? What about Geezer Ghetto? If it were as Nick described, it was built on fantasy. How about Elder Disney World?

I hit the steering wheel with my palms. "What if he assaulted some poor old lady? What if he flashed someone?"

"What if nothing you fear happened? What if they love him?" asked Joyce. Bonnie nodded in agreement.

"You two are betting on Nick. I am betting this Andrea has never heard of sundowners. I am about to be embarrassed beyond belief."

"So who's the narcissist now?" Another damning throwaway from Joyce. She opened the door.

"Well...."

"It's not about *you*, is it, dear?" Bonnie put a period on the conversation.

We got out of the car and approached the entry. Joyce took my arm. "Come on. His program is obviously important to him, and if it is as Nick says, they'd want to know what's happening with him."

Here we were, and there it was: the willful suspension of disbelief. "Is he or isn't he the life of the party, the energizer bunny, the prime candidate for a grant?" Joyce whispered.

"What if every bit of it is true?" Bonnie turned to me. "I'm prepared to be a believer. Are you prepared to be wrong?" It was the most direct thing she had said to me.

"We'll see," I replied, and I pushed the doorbell.

"Just a minute," said a cheerful voice on the intercom.

A woman I guessed to be in her early thirties opened the door to greet us. "Hi. I'm Andrea." She wore jeans, a coral sweater, a big smile. Of course, the lovely Andrea. That part of Nick's fantasy was true. She pumped our hands with a firm grasp.

"I'm Ben, Nick's brother."

"Is something wrong? Where's Nick?" She was watching me carefully. In this business, one had to be hard-wired for tragic or life-altering news delivered without sham. Before I could introduce Bonnie and Joyce, she made it a demand: "Is he *okay*?"

"He's in the hospital, Andrea. I had Nick out for an evening in the city with my friends, Bonnie and Joyce, who live here...."

Joyce and Bonnie said their hellos.

"I'm so happy to meet all of you. Nick was so excited you were coming, Ben."

"He told you I was coming?"

"Absolutely. What did he call it? Oh yes—a 'millennial event.' He couldn't stop talking about you."

Maybe he had forgiven me for staying away. But—he couldn't stop talking about me?

"What happened? Tell me!"

"He had a diabetic reaction to some old beer we didn't know was in a cupboard. He drank a lot of it."

She put her hand on her heart. "Is it serious?"

"They think he'll pull through. He should be out today or tomorrow if everything goes okay. But you know, with everything else, the odds aren't great."

"If anything happens to Nick, it will be a terrible loss for Elder Town. He has been part of us for ten months, but it's more like ten years…oh, come in, come in, meet some of our guests. I want to tell them about Nick."

I could only guess how my face looked. Bonnie and Joyce looked smug. We followed Andrea into a good-sized clubroom full of scattered armchairs, card tables with ergonomic-looking folding chairs, a ping pong table, and, in the center of the room, a large table. For group projects and probably meetings. Bookshelves packed with books and magazines lined an entire wall. Wood plank floors looked good for dancing. In the corner stood a burnished upright piano.

It was indeed Nick's kind of place.

Andrea stood at the piano and played a few chords. The two dozen elders stopped the card-table chatter.

"Nick's in the hospital," Andrea announced. There were cries of "Oh no" from those who could hear and "Who?" from those who couldn't. I suspected that announcements like this were part of the daily routine. Andrea repeated the announcement in a louder voice. Some guests registered alarm, but kept right on dealing cards and calling bingo numbers. Elder Townspeople pursued being alive.

"This is his brother, Ben. And meet Bonnie and Joyce, their friends." Bonnie waved and Joyce smiled. People clapped.

"That the brother who never left the farm?" shouted one lady.

"No, he's the teacher too busy to visit," hissed another.

Good old Nick had planted pungent character assassinations here. I was the self-absorbed rustic from the plains.

It didn't take long for the testimonials to Nick to spill out. A man rose from his easy chair and shook his finger at me. "That brother of yours, he gets me up off my ass and gets me dancing with the ladies. Keeps me alive." He shook his head and sat back down. "What'll I do if he dies?"

A woman spoke quietly in Spanish to another woman sitting alongside her.

"What did Rosita say?"

"She says Nick is a Latin lover. He comes up to her and tells her she is '*muy especiale*' and pretty soon she's dancing the tango!" Rosita, the woman who spoke only Spanish, was blushing. There was laughter joined by lots of murmured "yeahs."

My claim that Nick was totally deluded was being cruelly dismantled. Bonnie was smiling radiantly, and Joyce kept rolling her eyes. Surely the bad stuff about Nick would come out, too.

A sharp-featured woman with hands that trembled set down her bridge hand, adjusted her bra straps and launched out in a window-rattling voice. "Your brother taught us about sundowning, young man. He changed our *lives!*" I feared this one, a true clairvoyant who intuited my dismissal of Nick as a fraud. I didn't like the way I was feeling at all. She went on.

"You should have been here long ago to see how far we've come with sundown nights. We are pioneers here at Elder Town, and Nick is...well, he's the wagon master. I've had more fun at this place in one night than I ever had in all the years of my marriage, including in bed."

An amazing number of people clapped and chimed in, "Oh, yeah!" A few others guffawed.

"Wait a minute!" came a wizened male voice from the bookshelves. "I'm her husband." Everyone laughed.

The woman continued. "None of us knew why we or our spouses were scared when nighttime was coming on, the sun going down over those beautiful hills out there. Especially the loopy ones. They'd get so ornery and antsy around five in the afternoon, it took three nurses to hold one of them down. All we knew was we were taking pills for this and that, and we were feeling sorry for ourselves. And then Nick got this sundowners program going." Her voice cracked. "He better not desert us now."

"I'm with her!" said a large woman, whose feet were planted atop a newspaper lying on the floor. Her dress was short. Her veined and puffy legs showed from above her knees down to her orthopedic shoes. "We paint, we make pots, we dance, we get massages, we listen to that Mozart guy and all the great singers." She paused and a glint shone from her eyes. "And some of us talk dirty to each other!"

"Ooh la la, that Nick!" shouted the trembling woman. She slammed down a fist and sent her bridge hand flying.

"Sometimes we all go to a late-night restaurant that Nick likes," chirped a small lady in a wheelchair. "Nick introduced us to tapas. Wow! I shut my eyes when I eat them."

A woman whose back was bent from osteoporosis moved toward us. "The best is when he plays the bass fiddle, and a piano player from San Mateo shows up," She said. "Andrea fixed up a light that spins. We move, we move, we *move!*" Her voice rose higher and her back seemed to straighten with each "move."

A hunched-over man sitting near a window rubbed his neck and said, "I love the smell of incense, I love the feel of somebody's hands gently rubbing my back."

A woman with clear blue eyes who was sitting close to him took him by the hand. They started singing a duet of "Irene, Good Night." Soon, almost everyone in the room was up singing the tune, arm in arm, swaying back and forth. They pulled the three of us and Andrea into the circle. It all lasted maybe five minutes.

Afterwards, everyone found a place to sit and it was quiet for a few seconds as the guests retrieved their breath.

"And we open up and confess all!" shouted another lady. Everything about her was big: hair, lips, eyes, arms, breasts, torso. "Nick gets us going and pretty soon I'm talking about an affair I had fifty years ago after my drunken husband beat me up. And I'm telling people about early boyfriends I hadn't remembered for years. Like Gary Snodgrass. He was so shy I had to wrap a scarf around his neck to make him kiss me. Damn near choked him to death," she giggled. "I should have stuck with him."

"And then we are ready for bed," another woman said. "Nick reads to us. Usually a short story or a poem. Or something about modern love in that New York City newspaper. And most of us fall into a sleep so deep we don't hear anything until the next morning."

No pills, no meds. Just Nick.

Lovely Andrea's face shone like a horizon moon. Bonnie was grinning now, like she had known all along that Nick was not all snake oil. Joyce kept her cool but her lower lip quivered a bit.

"Hey," shouted the same guy who had started the testimonials. I noticed Andrea stiffening. "Nick is a genius. Those late night parties—well, here's the thing—I love the girls, but never could see how I could get close to them. Well, you should see me at sundown! I've had some pretty good...."

"Thanks, everybody," Andrea cut him off. "We'll remember Nick in everything we do today." She led the three of us out of the room to the sound of clapping.

On the way to the front door, Joyce asked in a cozy, innocent-sounding voice, "Andrea, does Nick try to seduce you—well, or anyone?"

Andrea blushed. "Every day! Mostly he just holds me tight when we're dancing, and says, 'Let's run away—don't care where! Even Bismarck, No-Dak!'" She looked knowingly at me. "Is it fun there, Ben?"

"Not that I've noticed," I said.

Everybody laughed, and I finally did too.

"I tell my boyfriend every single thing Nick says, everything he does. I tell him he could learn a lot from Nick." She looked at me and sighed. "You can see how everyone here feels.

He's more than the life of the party. He is the *soul* of the party. My job would be twice as hard without him. And it's twice as much fun with him."

"And the county says this nighttime stuff is okay?" I asked.

"Absolutely."

"Has anyone died after one of these all-nighters?" I was still incredulous.

She smiled. "People die all the time around here. Whenever someone dies the day after sundown, someone always says, 'We sent her out in style' or 'May God bless him and bring him home to the big party in the sky.'"

Bonnie took Andrea's hand. "Nick's brother thinks he's delusional, grandiose. Do you see any of that?"

Andrea hooted. "Of course! But with Nick, like with everyone else here, we try to take the good and discard the useless. Nick's a treasure here."

"Would Elder Town welcome a grant to develop the program?" asked Bonnie.

That stopped the bubbling Andrea cold. She looked straight at Bonnie. "Are you kidding? Sure we would! We get questions about it all the time. Nick is becoming famous in the geriatric community out here. The revels are known as Nick's Nights."

"We'll be in touch," said Bonnie. "Thanks."

"If you ever need a piano player, here's my card," Joyce said. Andrea hugged each of us. She stood at the doorway and waved as we walked toward the van.

"So. About Nick being delusional," said Joyce. "That was one hell of a delusion."

Bonnie just looked at me.

"It warrants further investigation," I said, more than a little lamely. "The guests could have felt compelled—what else could they say?"

They both laughed. "The truth," they said in unison. "They couldn't have planned that," said Bonnie.

Joyce added, "Of course not. They had no idea we were coming."

I *was* ashamed I found it so hard to accept the testimony of these people. Imperious asshole indeed. Just because they needed care, just because they were vulnerable, just because they could no longer live independent lives, I pre-listed every one of them as brainwashed by Nick, the master trickster. How easy it was to pigeonhole their testimonials as fanciful, pathetic attempts to hang on to normalcy.

The women said no more and I retreated into my thoughts as I drove. Okay, I've got my blind spots, and they just get more blinding as I age. Old people are like unemployed people. The longer a worker's unemployed, the tougher it is to get a job. The longer old people are in a home, the less in touch they are. I was labeling them the cute, useless generation. What had just happened surprised me, but I still wasn't ready to give Nick a pass. I had to admit, in this one brief encounter, the myths — *my* myths — were exploded. Old people in institutions actually talk about sex. Some of them like staying up late. They enjoy being physical. They still read books.

At the same time they had nailed my putdown of Nick. I had actually been chastened and humbled. I began to wonder what else had changed about Nick. If he *had* changed, I was sad it was at the end of his life, the end of our life as brothers.

This much was clear to me — Nick had no delusions about the revels of the night. He was parlaying his gift for the placebo effect into something that touched the hearts and the brains of the elders of Elder Town. My brother knew his neurochemicals all right.

"Don't take it too hard," said Bonnie. "Remember — find tears for the suffering of Nick."

I grumbled something. I was *not* a gracious loser. She meant, let his misfortune melt even *your* heart," but it felt like, "Get over it."

From Elder Town it was a short five-minutes up to Sunnyslope. I told Bonnie and Joyce that I dreaded this meeting. I suspected that Consuela would like nothing better than to be rid of Nick the nut cake and his well-meaning but blundering brother. As we pulled into the driveway, I warned them that Consuela might consider them guilty by association with me.

José opened the door. "Hi, Ben. Nick still in the hospital?" Before I could answer, he yelled to Consuela that Nick's brother was here. She came out of the kitchen looking both anxious and stern. José hovered behind the couch. I made introductions and summarized the story of Nick's collapse.

"Look, Consuela, I am *so* sorry. You've got to believe me. Joyce forgot she'd had old beer in the pantry. It was one of those things. We had not drunk alcohol the entire evening. We were playing music. Nick went to the bathroom and, well...."

Consuela looked at us wearily and for a split second I saw Nick through her eyes. Always a handful, he must have been especially hard to handle when he rolled in at seven a.m. after a sundowners' all-nighter, high on dopamine if nothing else.

"Your brother, he is a character." José broke the ice. "He likes the beer. He's always on the lookout when I take him to the dentist or somewhere. I make sure he has no money. Even without any beer—when he comes home after Elder Town, he is ready to dance and sing. I got to work real hard to get him into bed."

Consuela nodded.

Bonnie started chatting with Consuela in Spanish. Consuela rattled off a torrent of words that I knew, based on her glances, contained deep concerns not only about Nick, but also about me.

I leaned forward. "This will never happen again," I blurted out. I gave Consuela Dr. Sharma's card and assured her he would be in touch with San Mateo County Medical Services.

She said nothing. "Consuela, I want to keep Nick here. You've been so good to him."

Just then Frieda entered from the kitchen and I introduced her to the women. Behind her came the smell of bread just out of the oven. Whiffs of corn tortillas and the cooking of raw onions, cilantro, lime, and tomatoes spread out into the living room. She wiped her hands on her apron and smiled nervously. I hoped we could stay long enough to eat.

Consuela finally spoke. "Ben, I worry the county will find out about Nick's misbehavior and call me in. 'Consuela, what is this we hear about Nick, that you let him go out and drink alcohol, and he got sick and went to the hospital. Now we must....'" She smiled but it was ominous. "We maybe get shut down." José looked alarmed.

"I'll see his case worker tomorrow, I'll explain it was all me. I promise." I took her hands and squeezed them.

A telephone jangled. José went to answer it.

"Ben, it's a doctor from the hospital." Conversations stopped. Consuela crossed herself.

"He just walked out," Dr. Sharma barked into the receiver. "There was a Code Blue at the adjoining station. All the docs and nurses dropped what they were doing and ran. Nick happened to be walking in the hallway, the last anyone remembered. No one saw him leave. He just disappeared in the confusion."

"Oh my god," I said. Consuela was staring right through me. "You have to be joking. Tell me you're joking," I begged the doctor, and whispered to the others, "He's gone AWOL."

"Give them my cell phone number," Joyce said.

Sharma spoke over my whisper, "Where do you suggest the police start looking for your brother?"

I didn't have to think long: "Haight Street and Golden Gate Park." He gave me the phone number of a cop on the case.

I faced Consuela and stuttered out the news. There were frantic exclamations in Spanish between her and Frieda. José toyed nervously with the TV remote. I promised we'd find Nick and bring him home. I couldn't wait to drag Joyce and Bonnie out to the van.

Bismarck looked really good to me right now. No bay, no ocean, no Land's End, no mad, evasive brother on the run. Just the muddy Missouri flowing steadily by, circling through the country's midsection after many failed starts and stops out west on its steady way south and east to meet the Mississippi. In Bismarck, everything followed the beat of "Ah one, ah two, ah three," as our orchestra leader Lawrence Welk from little Strasburg, North Dakota, used to count on national TV. We knew where we were in the waltz of time and how many beats were in the measure. Out here it was one improv note after another. And sometimes it was cacophony.

I was out of my depth with my brother, Captain Chaos.

"That sonofabitch!" I'd missed the entry to Highway 101. "How the hell do you get out of this town?" I was so rattled I'd taken two wrong turns.

Joyce was fidgeting with a map. "Where to?"

"I have this feeling he is heading for Land's End."

Joyce poked at the map "Great. Where would that be? Ocean Beach?"

"That's it. With Nick it was Land's End this and Land's End that, all the time. He was never interested in the bay side of town. He wanted to be where the ocean met the land. The Great Highway and Ocean Beach."

"Even greater," said Joyce, rolling her head back on the head-rest. "Miles and miles of beach, block after block of three-story apartment or condo buildings. Oh my god. We have to corner this guy but there are no corners. The jerk!" She started laughing. Bonnie joined her. I gave in. They were right. It was beyond bizarre.

Joyce produced a bulky black cell phone from her bag. "We ought to call the cops and tell them our location." We were in luck. Neither Bonnie nor I owned one. Joyce dialed the police number I'd been given.

"For years he lived in an apartment on the Great Highway. He called it Land's End Aloft. I think I can find the block. I just can't remember the address." Joyce's phone rang—police requesting more information. She put it on speakerphone. "The hospital has reason to be concerned," one cop said confidentially before he hung up. "An escaped patient wearing a doctor's jacket. This could really embarrass them." Credit Nick for that little flourish, I thought—the entire medical staff outwitted by a patient—a clinical psychologist.

A half-hour later we were cruising down the Great Highway. Behind the sand dunes to our left lay Ocean Beach. Slowing to a crawl, we left the expressway and drove north on the parallel highway until we took a right at a local street and parked. We piled out and walked quickly back to the highway. Stucco residences lined up side by side, each one distinguished by sand-caked windows that looked out at the dunes beyond the expressway. Rusting iron gates protected stairways to second and third floors. Baghdad by the briny sea, in Nick's words.

Any of them could have been Nick's Land's End Aloft. Which was his? I squirmed. I had been on this street before, but it was a long time ago. I surveyed the houses in both directions. The afternoon sun glinted off the windows and drained color from the facades, rose to pink, coral to peach. Somewhere along here Nick used to fix his eyes on the Pacific, curse nightfall and dial North Dakota.

This was Land's End, ultimate sundown, where Nick channeled the biblical Joshua who wanted to make the sun stall and slip its orbital path. In Nick's world, old people need not fear the terrors of the night because there would be no night.

Several blocks later, we walked past the Noriega Street intersection. I knew we were close to his place but I was still stuck without the address. Joyce phoned the police about our location. No word on Nick. They wanted to know if he was suicidal—could he have just gone over a dune somewhere and walked serenely into the tide? Joyce relayed the question to me. I said no. But I wondered if he felt humanistic psychology had failed him now, or he it. "Failed lives," he had mumbled at Joyce's condo Monday night before he collapsed. In his eyes, was his life one of them?

We had no choice but to cross the dunes. He loved to walk on Ocean Beach. He used to tramp around in the sand, with a funny little shuffle that looked like a slow-motion jog in quicksand. "Thank god for the white coat," I said. "If he's on the beach, he'll stand out."

We retreated and crossed at Noriega Street. A berm on the ocean side of the highway served as a median between the expressway and the highway. Now and then I spotted tiny, hardy white flowers nestled in the green and red ground cover. Joggers and stroller-pushers jostled with bicyclists for passage on an adjacent path. For a moment I expected Nick to stroll by.

A traffic light stopped the blur of automobiles and trucks on the Great Highway, and we trudged over the dune and down to the beach just as the sun edged into the horizon. Shadows of joggers and hikers were elongated across the ridges of sand. The surf banged in, and slunk out. Whitecaps blossomed like stars. A distant solitary freighter sailed out to sea. We looked up and down the beach. No Nick.

Joyce suggested we go north toward Golden Gate Park. That made sense. She called the police dispatcher and gave them our location. The officer said police were already starting out from the Park and sweeping the beach walking south. We started north.

As we walked, I talked. I told them about my last really friendly time with Nick. It was in 1976—the bicentennial year of the Declaration of Independence. Jeanne Marie and I had taken Clare and Frances to San Francisco over the July Fourth weekend.

He'd been fairly sane then, inquisitive about my life, not yet falling-down drunk. And he'd had a job—at California

Veterans Health Services. While Jeanne Marie had fixed lunch or dinner in his apartment, Nick and I were on the beach with my daughters. I recalled Nick shouting, with arms swung wide and a cigarette clenched between his teeth.

"This, bro, this Land's End Aloft is where I lived during my greatest therapeutic successes and professional breakthroughs. And of course I scored numerous times in the apartment!" He'd paused for breath and rubbed his hands together while I'd moved us out of earshot of my daughters.

He and I had walked on the beach every day. He'd shout into the wind, "I must go down to the seas again, to the lonely sea and the sky." And if he'd guzzled a six-pack, he'd start intimidating people. I told Bonnie and Joyce about a couple huddled together near a small fire. When they'd heard Nick ranting, they moved closer together. Lone joggers and walkers had turned around to stare. I could still see their walking-backward footprints in the wet sand.

Now years later, here I was again, tromping along Ocean Beach in the fading light. Bonnie and Joyce let me go on talking. I told them how I told Nick about the feeling I had as a child that the planet was all land. After all, Bismarck is almost equidistant from both coasts. To me, water was river or wetland. My father sold real estate in Bismarck, and he loved the solid riverside buildings and homes that still graced the city at mid-century. I had embraced the North Dakota of my parents as ardently as Nick had discarded it.

My reveries about water always got Nick going about water beginning on California shores and circling the world, the kingdom of Oceania. He called Oceania eternal, while land lasted only until a tectonic plate moved, and then land was subducted, sunk and died. Land was where typhoons and hurricanes destroyed cities. But oceans were forever.

Lands End Aloft: his tectonic, erotic life kept Oceania at bay and held off eternity at the comfortable distance of a hundred yards, just beyond the dunes. Love lived at Land's End Aloft. Death was just across the street. This was what my brother thought. He cued up the world every day for the cyclical push and pull between love and death, dawn and nightfall.

The police had to be approaching from the north somewhere. Dusk was muddied by a rolling fog. How foolish to think we'd find him here. He could have caught a taxi at the hospital, met some street folks, and organized a séance on the beach. Or maybe, all alone, he'd had the cabbie drop him off somewhere, and in a dope-induced state had really walked into the ocean, his white doctor's jacket disappearing under the waves, one arm, one finger held high, conducting his last notes.

Bonnie was the first to see Nick through the suddenly enveloping fog. Fewer than fifty feet away, a circle of people sat nursing a tiny fire pit of branches and sticks. As we got closer, I could see they were all listening to a man wearing a white medic's coat, collar pulled tight around his neck.

"Your mystical brother," uttered Bonnie.

"Just what I envisioned, surrounded by stoners," whispered Joyce.

I couldn't help but laugh.

We walked until we were twenty feet from Nick. The horizontal slant of the sun's rays through the fog had turned the surface of the sand into a bumpy, brittle moonscape. Sundown.

Through a brief clear patch in the fog, a small force of police closing in from the north. Joyce scowled. "Oh my god! They'll treat him like a fugitive for impersonating a doctor."

We got to him first, but only by a minute. The waves crashed, the fog closed in, the sparks from the fire sputtered. The cops from the north held back in the darkness, waiting for the three of us to make the first move.

"Nick?" I interrupted him in mid-sentence.

He looked confused. "Nick. You okay?"

Then he perked up. "Hey, welcome to the circle. Got firewood? Somebody left this little hearth aglow, and my brothers and sisters and I fed it with twigs and stuff, whatever we could find. Rustle up some goddamn firewood. It's cold, baby, but Land's End is alive!"

He didn't recognize us in the fog. Nick was seated, cross-legged. He was holding up his arm, hand pointed to the sky, one finger extended. Teaching the multitudes. We edged closer. The group consisted of men and women, all with that curious bronze sheen, hair and skin an identical color. All visibly stoned. They were passing two joints around. Nick inhaled deeply when one came to him, finger still up in the air. He hung on as long as he could and then let the smoke out slowly. His voice rose.

"From World-War-Two Europe, Rollo May brought existentialism and phenomenology. It was the right time, America needed him. Humanistic psychology was becoming Mary-Poppins-ish, poppin-ish, whatever. All too goody-two-shoes. Humanistic psych needed to recognize the presence of evil, the tragedy that hangs over us all. The failed lives, the failed societies. You all know the scene, right?" There were grunts from around the circle. I felt like we were intruding on a Stonehenge group therapy session, men and women sharing weed and grooving on the words of a shaman.

"Nick!" My voice hung in the air, midway between a shout and a cry. "It's Ben." Startled, Nick looked over in our direction again. He started shaking. His face turned red with an emotion I couldn't decipher. He slunk down low.

The circle of potheads was his bulwark against the sober world. "What's up, brother?" he asked in a cold, distant voice.

"I've been looking for you."

"And you've found me. Now go away."

Here and there faces in the circle turned to look at Bonnie, Joyce and me. I didn't think any of them would try to stop me from taking Nick away. They seemed too stoned to get physical. But the last thing I wanted was the three of us getting into a free-for-all before the police closed in.

Bonnie was shaking when she addressed Nick. "We'd like you to go with us to Joyce's. We're having a party."

"And you would be...?" He was higher than I'd thought.

"She would be the angel of fucking mercy!" shouted one of the men in the circle. "Go with them and bring back beer."

"Fuck that noise!" Nick was getting into his hostile self now.

"It's Bonnie. Remember me? And Joyce? Stern Grove? Haydn's *Creation*?

"Go on, man, bring back a truckload of Coors," yelled one of them. "Bring Hayden too!"

Then I saw police lights flashing from the Great Highway. The potheads saw them too and their bodies stiffened like seabirds interrupted at scavenging. The law, the most powerful critter in the food chain, was coming on strong.

Evidently, stoned people scatter fast. Only Nick remained in the center, arm still erect, and finger still pointing heavenward. The master still taught, never mind that the disciples had scuttled off in twos and threes down to the wet sand of the shoreline. A burly male cop and a tall female cop approached us, both brandishing flashlights. The female pointed to Nick's medic jacket and approached him quietly. The male cop spoke first.

"Okay, your name?"

"Who the fuck wants to know?" Nick said. Oh, the adroit timing of his Socratic response.

"The San Mateo police want to know. If you are Nick, we would like you to come with us."

The female cop looked at me after checking a sheath of papers. "You Ben?"

"Yes."

She nodded to Bonnie and Joyce and then looked back at me. "We have been told to bring him back to Saint Francis Memorial. Will you meet us there? You have transportation?"

"Yes. Of course."

Nick had gradually lowered his arm down to his side. A bite-size joint lay on the sand a few feet away. He stood, sidestepped over to it and covered it with his bare feet. He grabbed a small branch from the sand. "I want to call my attorney," he said.

"We are not arresting you. We could, though, with that joint lying under your foot," growled the male cop.

"It's medicinal. I have blinding migraines and chronic pain. Doctor's prescription." Nick stood by the fire pit and poked at the embers with the branch.

"We will arrest you on two charges: impersonating a doctor and vagrancy, unless you come with us now, Nick."

"Ask my brother if I'm a vagrant." He swung toward me. "And I am a doctor! I don't impersonate doctors. I *am* one!"

The cop looked at me. An old fear paralyzed me. "He's a psychologist," I said. And he's sick and I abandoned him—I left all that unsaid.

Nick stoked the embers, daring the police to take him. A sudden memory kindled in me—us, in our twenties, at home. We were outside grilling hamburgers. Smoke rose in our faces as the burgers sizzled on the rack. We argued about predestination and free will. It was as if, despite our different interests, we cared about the same core things in life.

"You okay?" Joyce asked. "You don't look so good."

"For the first time in decades, I miss the brother I grew up with." I kept the memory to myself. The details didn't matter.

"They're taking him to the hospital. Better pay attention," Joyce said, sounding worried.

I walked over to Nick and hugged him. This time I meant it. I took the branch from his hand. "I love you, Nick," I whispered. "I'll see you at the hospital."

Nick stared at me through red-rimmed eyes.

"Where do you live, Doctor?" The female cop approached Nick slowly. She had a quiet but forceful demeanor.

"I live in San Mateo. Sunnyslope Manor. I'm retired from the service of mankind. Do you want to thank me for my service?"

"Right. I *do* thank you. You can go home after the hospital, Doc. My name's Carla."

"Carla the Jackal?" he snorted.

She smiled. "Been called worse. Why don't you let me give you a hand back to the van? I think you could use a little R and R." She reached out her hand to him. He looked at it for a few seconds, then at me.

"Brother, is this the kind of love you want to show ol' Nick? You let these Fascists drag me away?" I felt weak in the knees. Bonnie walked over to Nick and held out her hand from the side opposite the policewoman's. Nick looked at Bonnie through bloodshot eyes, then went limp. The two women grabbed his arms and steadied him. The male officer came up and asked Bonnie to step aside. She did. He took Nick's arm, slung it over his shoulder and propped Nick up. Carla grabbed Nick around the waist and threw her other arm over his shoulder and the two of them carried him over the dunes. Nick didn't resist.

In a few minutes, their flashing lights on the Great Highway moved off to the east. Except for a few embers in the fire pit, it was completely dark on the beach.

From all around us, like hulking gorillas returning to their camp after hiding from poachers, the members of the circle trudged back. They reminded me of silent monks filing into chapel to chant vespers. They sat down cross-legged and started passing around another joint that one of them had rolled during the standoff between Nick and the police. Life went on.

"Want some weed?" a woman asked Joyce through blistered lips. Life went on.

Joyce smiled at her. "No thanks."

A man whose face was lined and gristled said, "You know there are three waves in twentieth century psychology, right?" They had heard the lecture.

"Yeah, I was aware of that. Pretty neat, eh?"

"Yeah. So, tell Nick not to forget the Coors. Coors is the fourth wave." There was loud laughter. The waiting police from the north approached the circle and began rounding people up.

The three of us hiked back to the van and drove to Saint

Francis. Once again the medics had me fill out a ton of forms. I emptied my pockets of every scrap of information I had about Nick. I put them in touch with his social worker in San Mateo County. When Dr. Sharma finally sat down with us, it was close to eight.

"I'm glad your brother is back. I apologize for everything."

"You say that like I don't know how impossible it is to control him." I wanted Sharma to know I appreciated his kindness to Nick.

"The dude that eludes," quipped Joyce.

Sharma laughed. He looked grateful we were not angry at the hospital. "Here is what happened. One of our docs had taken off his coat to help perform CPR on a patient in a nearby room. He tossed it over a chair in the nurse's station. In the confusion, nobody saw Nick take the doc's coat. He went back to his room and dressed himself, shoes, shirt, and pants. He walked out and took a stairway down to the lobby. Nobody saw him leave the unit. He waved to staff at the front desk."

He paused and chuckled. "Nothing funny here of course. But at the hospital entrance he passed a nurse just coming on duty. According to her, Nick said something like, 'Hello, I'm new on staff here. Are you free after work tonight?'"

"Trying to score as usual," I muttered.

Sharma attempted a smile. "Well, she was shocked and said no, she was not free. Then he said he needed twenty-five dollars for a cab and he would pay her back tomorrow. Everything about him looked and sounded suspicious, except for the medic's name on the badge. He pointed to it and covered the mug shot above. She gave him money.

"As soon as she checked in at her station, she started asking around about dating culture here. Someone called the real doc, who by the way is married and the father of five, and he immediately contacted the nurse. She was stunned. So we knew Nick was missing within five minutes, but didn't know how he got out until the doc started to ask about his jacket and the new nurse told us her story."

he says this constantly.

"Welcome to Nick's world," I said. I told him how Nick the teenager tied me up in knots because he could talk faster than I. He tricked me out of my allowance, stole my cigarettes. "He comes by these skills naturally," I said. Sharma grinned.

"How bad is his medical condition this time?" The three of us leaned in closer. Sharma said Nick would not die from marijuana but from diabetes, from his system going into toxic shock after not taking insulin. Or his heart, scarred and enlarged, might give out any time. He might die tonight or two months from now. He asked whether they should resuscitate if he stopped breathing. I said my brother was a ward of the state but they had my vote. No. The doctor said they'd keep Nick overnight before deciding on what to do next.

We were allowed into his room for a brief moment. He was hooked up to an IV, and an oxygen mask covered his mouth. Bonnie kissed his forehead. Joyce tousled his hair. He couldn't open his eyes or his mouth. For the first time in my life I missed his bright repartee. I put my hand over his free one. "You bastard, don't die on me. We have things to talk about."

Bonnie and Joyce picked up Joyce's car in the hospital ramp. I was happy to be alone, to follow the two of them back to Joyce's place. The day's images were scrambled in my brain: Nick's fan club at Elder Town, the phone call from Sharma, the search on Ocean Beach, the circle of addicts around the dying embers. My sudden memory of us as teenagers. Three days ago, my world had collided with Nick's and I now was firmly in his erratic orbit—a place I vowed I'd never be. I was ready for a drink. The irony didn't escape me.

After we parked and went upstairs, we all headed for the separate showers. Joyce found jeans and a shirt that belonged to one of her sons and threw my clothes in the washer.

Clothes. I needed to buy clothes.

I called Consuela from the phone in the study. For the second day in a row, I apologized. Consuela sounded resigned to whatever happened. "I am praying for your brother, and so are Frieda and José. Even Barney and the others bowed their heads at supper tonight. That bad boy, that Nick!" I said I hoped he would be back home in a day or two. Back together, like before I showed up. Didn't say that last part out loud.

I returned to the living room. Bonnie was drinking wine, Joyce had a whiskey. "I'll take one of those," I said, pointing to Joyce's glass. I toasted them. "Without you two, it'd just be me alone in some bar. Thank you for not checking out—which, of course, you should have." We clinked glasses and sipped.

Joyce sighed. "So there is this thing called sundowning. It scares the hell out of me. I'm full of end-of-day anxiety at this very moment just thinking about it!"

She shook her head as if she was warding off the onset of a sundowner. "You know...well, okay, here's my take on the day's lessons. Nick's sundowning is really about men, isn't it? Men get crazy at night, always have. Out they go, out for the evening, full of fantasy. Women tend the hearth, clean the dishes, and put the little ones to bed. Don't even notice the sun going down. Men hunt the sun. Am I right? But most of the elders are women. I don't get it."

"Give the gender thing a break, Joyce," I frowned. "Apparently sundowning doesn't discriminate."

She was undeterred. "Maybe men get it first and then transmit it to women much later. I mean, men get sour, negative. They decide the person by their side is not the caring, loving woman they married. Of course not! The woman they married was somebody who would take care of them and adore them and whoa, here she is, having only raised three kids, just another human being with her own needs." She pounded the cushions for emphasis. "It's not about sex, no matter what they say. It's about being nursed! Men get sour, bitching about this and that, weather and sports and kids—oh, especially the kids.

They want no part of a domesticity that includes equal responsibility for the kids! They just want to go out for the evening. Every evening!"

Bonnie was watching the two of us. "I think, Joyce, you and I have a limited set of experiences with men. I do, anyway."

Joyce paused, emptied her glass and forged ahead. "Listen, my ex needed a nurse, somebody who would be there as he lay suffering on the couch after his workday. For Christ's sake, he had a cushy job in a law firm! They loved him. When he came home the expectation was clear: feed him, satisfy him and accompany him as the good wife. And he goes and gets sour! About what? About everything! Nothing too small. The crummy weather. The stock market. The dirty kitchen. Our sex life." She poured another whiskey for herself. "Help yourself," she said to me.

"When the nurse-wife finally rebels and walks out, Mister Man finds somebody else to do her job. It's the male fantasy, they can't help it, poor boys. Their genes tremble the very moment a woman begins to rebel against being caretaker-in-chief. They up and get rid of her and find a perfect—aka younger—mate for their golden years. And then they finally—usually—have the decency to die before her. And thanks to whatever money they leave her, she can, late in life—with a clear conscience—have her own needs and desires. Before dementia gets her."

"How long were you...." I started to ask.

"You're right. I'm generalizing from my own marriage. It took me only ten years to figure out I was there to care for the boy, just as his mommy had done before me. Another child in addition to the ones he and I had."

"Oh hell, we're all sundowners," Bonnie protested "It's not gender, it's regret—for wasted opportunities. The road taken ends in regret for the one not taken."

Joyce seemed to puzzle over that for a few seconds. "Sorry, it's gender, no matter which road is taken. Women go sundowning at Elder Town because some guy took mostly wrong turns over the years and now they're left with the car and nowhere to go."

Bonnie jumped up and waved her wine glass at us. "I think sundown anxiety starts the first time future prospects look dim compared to the past. Consider me."

"Yes, some consideration please," Joyce laughed and clapped.

Bonnie put on a very funny face, eyebrows lifted, teeth bared, mouth pulled wide open with her fingers. "I do whine, don't I?"

"You didn't get sour. You dealt with it," Joyce said. "You decided to leave the convent when you looked ahead and saw a *lonely* old age—alone, without a partner. You did not want to go gentle into that night, thank you, Dylan, and hooray for Bonnie."

I stared at Bonnie. "You didn't leave for a man, right?" She seemed uncertain how to answer.

"No." It was a singsong no. "I left for me, mostly. I've fantasized about marriage, but I've also had reality therapy from Joyce. 'Not at all what it's cracked up to be,' she kept shouting at me." Bonnie had Joyce's definitive bark down to a fine edge. "'On its own, at your age, definitely not worth leaving behind three square meals a day and lifetime security and the company of a few women friends you can trust.' That was her advice until a year ago. Until she was sure I was over menopause." Joyce gave a vehement nod. Bonnie took a sip of wine and sat down.

"I stayed in lots longer than my friends. As I told you the other day, they all left years ago, many, many married priests, had kids. A few formed lesbian unions and adopted. Others stayed single and some of them adopted too. I stayed. I wanted to experience change from inside the convent. We got rid of the habits, we lived in apartments, and we took on new ministries. It was good. Not great, but good. The order was adaptable, I thought. What I wasn't ready for was how the change was just on the surface. The longer I stayed, the more shadowy the whole vocation seemed. We were encouraged to have relationships with men as long as they were not...romantic, you know, sexual. It was all so ambiguous. 'Non-genital intimacy' they called it. Can you believe that?"

"Happy talk is what that was!" chortled Joyce.

"It sounds like something Nick might prescribe for couples in their nineties," I added.

Bonnie nodded. "Talk about naiveté. Not many people are called to celibacy but even fewer can be somehow intimate and stay non-genital. I have nothing but admiration for the women who can live with the ambiguity and with the huge personal needs of the priests with whom they are intimate. I couldn't."

"So you're not just making stuff up about Notre Dame."

She laughed. "Oh, not at all! Notre Dame nursed clerical and religious romances because the summer school of theology attracted nuns and priests and brothers like bees to honey. A chaste midnight kiss with a priest at the Grotto of Our Lady below the golden dome could quickly result in a marriage proposal. Or worse. There was more action at the grotto than on the football field!"

Joyce hooted. "Go Bonnie!" Joyce reached for the phone and ordered a pizza delivery. "Care what kind?" she asked us. Bonnie and I shook our heads no.

Bonnie refilled her glass and laughed with utter abandon, no trace anymore of the reserved ex-nun. "You would not believe the sexual immaturity of clergy! It just came out of hiding during those years." She drew close to me. "One priest called me on the phone to tell me that his religious order had just dedicated a new pipe organ in the monastic chapel. The technical church term for dedicating a pipe organ was erection. A sign went up on the bulletin board: 'The formal erection of the abbot's organ will be at 11 o'clock today. The pipes will be humming. Be there.'"

I laughed hard. She pressed her hand on my arm. "But when he told me the same story three nights running, I figured he had a problem. There were many lonely men in rectories looking for love. Still are."

"In all the wrong places," added Joyce.

"The clerical pedophile scandals were the last straw for me. I had my own issues of denial, but when the entire hierarchical edifice of the church was shown to be built on denial—and complicity—that was it."

I figured Bonnie and Joyce had shared stories like this many times. Joyce just nodded knowingly.

"Joyce came to the convent and took me to lunch, almost exactly a year ago. She said...."

"Here is what I said, verbatim," Joyce cut her off. "Bonnie, get out of there. I liked you better in the old days, when you knew what you were doing. Now you're like a wife in a loveless marriage, watching the years slip away, putting up with timid men talking about sex like teenagers on the telephone. Get out of there, babe! Write a book about the changing sisterhood and you. Go through adolescence. Get laid! Meet the real somebody or meet nobody. Grow old not too far away from me. You've got family money—enjoy it. Join the human race."

"The immortal words of Joyce," Bonnie said. "And that is precisely the moment I began to see I could help Joyce too." She leaned forward on the couch. "Mom and Dad were looking to move; they didn't even know a real estate agent. They asked me, and then...."

"...then they threw me a lifeline," Joyce said, with that impish grin she could infuse with hidden meaning. "Their house sold for five million. And they gave me a list of friends who were also looking to downsize." She shrugged her shoulders and repeated slowly, "They threw me a lifeline."

"What about your ex?" I asked.

"Look, he was a good provider. He was not a drunk. On the other hand, he ran around. I knew it for a long time and wanted to end our agony but I had no income of my own." Joyce stood and walked slowly around the room as if pushing a stone up a steep hill.

"It took me *years* to file for divorce. I was working for a nonprofit and getting my real estate license. When the day finally came when I knew I could make it and take care of my boys, when my husband bitched one more time about 'all the dirty dishes you store in the sink,' I pulled the plug on *him*!" She threw an imaginary plug over her shoulder. "And then it was touch and go for years. And then Sister Bonnie told me her parents wanted little old me to handle the sale of their big house in the most genteel neighborhood of San Francisco."

Bonnie took a large sip from her glass and set it down. "I feel ready for the world!"

"Here's the worst-kept secret about Bonnie," Joyce continued. "She's driven to do good. She will one day lead one of the best foundations in the country."

It struck me how easily women seemed to sustain deep friendships over a lifetime. I once thought that Nick and I would be that close. When it didn't turn out that way, it left me sad, restless, and sometimes those feelings surfaced, like tonight at Ocean Beach. I felt like I was drowning in landlocked North Dakota.

I wondered what would happen to their friendship if Bonnie went away and Joyce and I had a fling. There was a pretty strong sexual tension when the three of us were together. My thoughts flashed back to Jeanne Marie, when our sex life waned as her dependency grew. When a third force enters a relationship, things happen. Painkillers happened. And I still wondered, did Nick happen?

Joyce snapped her fingers a few times on one hand, then the other. "Oh this world with its male and female magnets that attract and repel, back and forth, back and forth. Can't live with, can't live without."

She pulled Bonnie up first, and then me. "Let's dance, people, before we melt in a puddle from soul-searching. If Nick is right, we can ward off sundowners by dancing our heads off."

She went to the stereo, selected a CD, and turned up the volume. "YMCA" blasted out of the speakers. I needed no encouragement and neither did Bonnie. The three of us boogied shoeless around the room, shouting the immortal four letters on cue and swinging our arms more or less in the flag sema-phore positions for Y, M, C, and A.

Joyce was a whirling demon. Bonnie exuded a mellow, floating joy. I sent them both into bursts of laughter when I confused the Y and M arm positions, something I used to do regularly as a chaperone at high school dances, much to the delight of the kids.

The pizza arrived. Mushroom, sausage, black olives and pepperoni. Joyce dimmed the lights and we ate looking out at the cathedral in the cool of the night. There was enough light to make out each other's faces.

"What are you thinking about?" Bonnie broke the quiet mood. "*Il Penseroso*, my friend."

I *was* pensive. What if her foundation...what if Nick achieved some recognition for helping people through the revels—would that success help him remember what passed between him and Jeanne Marie?

"It's about Nick, yes?"

I told her half the truth. "I'm thinking about you and your family's foundation. And how Nick might fit in. Tell me more about the foundation."

Bonnie summarized the developments that transpired about the time she left the convent. Her family was looking for new ways to help people in Ecuador. In the convent, she'd vol-unteered for a nonprofit that built compatible technology for villages in the developing world. Corn grinders, peanut butter processors, water purification systems. Her father asked her to come up with ways the foundation could take that program to the next stage.

She figured out what was still missing: Entrepreneurs in developing countries didn't have enough credit to get loans so they could obtain the materials and manufacture the hardware in their own country and not rely on stuff made in the U.S.

"Microfinance. It just kind of came together. I've been slowly reorganizing my life to start this new chapter. So my father has given five million dollars to a bank in Quito that we've chosen as a partner in a microfinance program. We will make microloans to local small-scale entrepreneurs. Mostly women. And we'll help them save money, too. Microsavings."

"And how long will you be in Quito?" I asked. They were right about my selfishness. All I could think of was that Nick needed support *now*.

"I'll be there for at least a month." She put her knees up to her chin. "I'm very excited about it. And you are looking at the *new* foundation president. Just decided."

"*That's* exciting," I enthused. "You're passionate about it, you've been a school superintendent. Shoot, you've *lived* in a nonprofit for decades. You'll be a terrific foundation executive."

She perkily acknowledged the compliment. "When Joyce and I met you and Nick, I knew I'd be leaving for Quito in a matter of weeks." She leaned her head against the back of the sofa. "I really wanted this brief little lark, Ben. And it *was* a lark: the ballet, Cliff House, Haydn's *Creation*. Exposure to sundowning. Twenty-four hours on the town. No agenda. I loved it. Now, it's another kind of adventure. Getting serious money over to Elder Town for research into the revels of the night. Not exactly a lark but maybe something deeper! I will pull foundation strings to make something happen." She reached out and touched my arm. "I can find some funds in a week, maybe two, just before I leave for Quito. We can *start* to eradicate that old devil sundown." In the darkness, her confidence sounded absolute.

Once again I woke up on Joyce's sofa bed. Joyce had folded my clothes and left them in the bathroom. I showered, dressed and made my way to the kitchen. Bonnie and Joyce were already there and immediately launched into a description of their strategy for the foundation grant. Neither of them had gone to bed right away. I poured myself some coffee and loaded a scone with raspberry jam while they talked.

They would feature the arc of Nick's life. When he emerged from being homeless and took up residence at Sunnyslope a year ago, he became a mythical hero, he pulled people with dementia off the junk heap of "senior citizenry" and made them loving, breathing, risk-taking people again. And he made use of other, healthier elders to be part of the rescue. Maybe it took someone with his personality, his training and his years of crazy living to create the revels. He built the model and others could take it from there.

Bonnie's scheme was believable enough. She saw it as a model that could be replicated elsewhere, all over the country. Most programs weren't prepared to deal with the thousands—millions of aging citizens. They're overwhelmed. No wonder they gave mounds of pills, just like Nick said. The grant would fund pilot programs, one for people with dementia, one for those without, but just living longer in some kind of care facility. The grant would cover the research, set up a baseline and a timeline. And it would look at the dark side, the fallout from the revels, the unintended consequences.

Wagging her index finger, Joyce discoursed on the demographics: So many more people living long into old age. We live longer, and we face impatient heirs fretting over shrinking inheritance, long hospitalizations, severely restricted activity and dreary nursing homes. It was an epidemic of quiet, untreated depression, often desperation. Nick put people in touch with something that helped them rise above it.

Here was Bonnie, the high school principal, the superintendent, the foundation president, the visionary. "Nick is the Good Samaritan, stopping on the road to bind up the wounds of the elderly whose human needs are ignored by others. It is so Catholic, it almost genuflects! What do you say, Ben?"

I had *never* thought of my brother as the Good Samaritan. "It's a terrific idea, but I'm afraid this good Samaritan will toss one 'motherfucker' into the middle of a foundation meeting and blow everything up. They'll want no part of this guy."

"He can be trained," Bonnie demurred.

I continued spouting reasons how the project could fail. In addition to curbing Nick's outbursts, I pointed out we'd need the okay of Andrea at Elder Town, and her boss, and whoever else ran the show. San Mateo County human services, endless bureaucracy. So many hoops. I excused myself and went to the bathroom.

When I came back, Joyce and Bonnie were on the balcony. It was a bright day and the cathedral was resplendent in the morning sun. They were chatting away.

"Finally, it will kill him, you know," I said.

"Maybe, maybe not," Joyce replied. "He's nearly died twice, once in Golden Gate Park, and yesterday on Ocean Beach. He might outlive us all."

"There's one more thing," I stepped out onto the balcony. "What your foundation will need to include is the power of the placebo effect."

"Nick never really explained that to us," answered Bonnie. "The heart of the matter, yes?"

It was. The placebo effect was the *sine qua non* of Nick's sorcery.

"Define it," Joyce said. Bonnie started scribbling notes.

"It's when some people experience a return to feeling better or even to good health because they believe they are receiving the right medical treatment." I paused for Bonnie to scribble.

Bonnie talked as she wrote. "It's usually when patients are given a sugar pill that they think is a powerful drug, right? And they experience a return to health."

The placebo effect had been part of my relationship with Nick for so long, I felt dizzy trying to simplify it.

I told them I had heard of questions about Valium—did it help decrease anxiety for people who didn't know the pill they were taking was Valium? There was suspicion that the drug didn't help in such cases. That was a different kind of placebo effect. I talked about a finding that some Parkinson's victims responded well to an injection of saline that they believed to be a drug. The saline not only diminished the symptoms of Parkinson's but also helped their bodies manufacture more dopamine—which Parkinson's destroys.

"Go figure," I said.

"So what's the connection to the revels?" asked Joyce. "Is it the dopamine rush Nick had at the Cliff House?"

"My take is that the revels' success relies on a different neurochemical. Twenty years ago, scientists discovered endorphins, substances that act like morphine or heroin. We produce and distribute these substances in the brain. When a trusted medical authority promises a patient relief from pain, even without a sugar pill, bingo, his brain produces endorphins. It's all chemicals."

Bonnie nodded. "What you're saying is that Nick promises relief from the pain of aging through the revels. Bingo, a whole bunch of elders start producing endorphins. And the effect lasts awhile—days, months? It doesn't have to be a pill. It's a promise made by someone the patient trusts. In this case, Doctor Nick. And patients no longer grow anxious at the end of the day."

"That's what your proposal is going to examine," I said. "And the foundation will want to know that there is an office of alternative medicine at the National Institutes of Health. That just happened recently—first time ever. Put that in the proposal. Studying the placebo effect is no longer studying snake oil medicine."

Joyce giggled. "Maybe we can bribe Dr. Sharma to serve as an advisor for the grant, in return for us keeping Nick's escape secret."

Bonnie and I laughed. "I'm not kidding!"

I finished off the last of the coffee. "I remain convinced that my brother is an imposter. I suppose you'd say I'm a victim of my own nocebos."

Bonnie took my hands in hers. She wore an earnest expression, and her voice was pleading. "Oh, Ben. More important than the grant is you and Nick. Don't leave without forgiving Nick. You came here angry with him. Don't leave...an angry man."

That's what it was about—she had it right.

Joyce leaned in. "Could you forgive Nick if you found out he had given your wife the pills that killed her?"

"I don't know." I had my car keys in hand. "For now, I'll play the empathetic brother. I'll *be* the empathetic brother."

Their physical closeness was having its effect. "You know, I've wanted to take him back to where he spent his last days before homelessness. His white-jacket escape from the hospital got in the way of that trip. Maybe we'll go to Fairfield after all. We'll look for his apartment, his fiddle, maybe even his Audi."

I felt lightheaded with these two. When I first came to the coast last Saturday, my body had done nothing but stand its ground and keep others at a distance. This kindness—and from strangers—was doing its work. Despite everything, I was feeling as relaxed as I'd been in a very long time.

I suspected I looked goofy as they watched me walk out into the hallway and ring for the elevator. For the first time in my life, forgiveness looked possible—desirable even.

The next two days were nonstop, head-to-head meetings with state and county social workers. I wanted them to know Nick had a family. They shared some files with me but I already knew most of his story from earlier phone conversations.

Evenings were with Nick at the hospital, sometimes meeting up there with Bonnie or Joyce. Back at my San Mateo B&B on Palm Avenue, I slept well and enjoyed leisurely breakfasts with *The New York Times* and the coverage of the turmoil in the royal family over Diana's death. I settled in. I found a Nordstrom in a nearby shopping center, and stocked up on under-wear, shirts and slacks. I found a dry-cleaner that did laundry.

I decided to go to a movie, and couldn't decide between *Ulee's Gold* and *The Full Monty*. I opted for the laughs. I took turns calling my daughters, updates every couple days. They wanted to talk about Princess Diana's and Mother Teresa's deaths so close to each other. I wanted to tell them about Bonnie and Joyce. I could imagine their phone calls after we hung up. "Can you believe Dad?" was no doubt the start of the conversation.

For Bonnie, the days were an assault on the usual timetable for submitting a grant. She and Andrea put a proposal together in forty-eight hours. Joyce, with a bonanza of two home sales, made almost as much in those three days as I did in an entire year of teaching, and she still found time to help Bonnie on the proposal. One night she went over to Sunnyslope to hobnob with Consuela and her crew, and with Barney, Rudy and Arnie on the front porch.

The hospital released Nick to a transitional care unit close to San Mateo. His vital signs were amazingly good, and he no longer needed oxygen. He was devouring real food. When I was with him, our conversation was sporadic, spliced in between his dozing and waking, but he was tracking.

"How's Andrea?" he asked.

"Outstanding. She says hello, and so do your friends at Elder Town. My god, these people love you."

"We get down at Elder Town."

"That sounds like the marinade of the ancient rhymer." I word-played. Nick liked word play. He grunted approval.

"And how is the lovely Bonnie?"

"I think she's okay. Haven't seen her for a couple of days."

"Well, get going, make hay. *Muy importante.*"

"Check."

"And herself, the nubile Numidian?"

"Joyful Joyce?" I checkmated. "Haven't seen a great deal of her either."

"You need me, bro, for the summit assault. You need me."

"About Land's End on the beach...." I fidgeted with my collar.

"Yes?"

"You were stoned out of your head."

"So they tell me. Sharma was as pissed off as he could be."

"No more pissed off than he was at your hospital escape."

"Well, I came around the corner, I saw the white jacket, and I conquered the system. *Veni, vidi, vici.*"

Not a hint of remorse.

At Sunnyslope, my conversations with Consuela and José were intense. I tried to convince them that they could still handle Nick and he did not need closer supervision or tighter restrictions. What they had to be thinking was that he needed *me* to go home. Consuela made it clear that both Nick and I were on probation.

The San Mateo facility released him and I brought him back home. Consuela and José came out to meet us as we turned into the driveway. José quickly opened the door to help Nick out. "Got a smoke?" Nick whispered.

"Nick, you are a naughty man," Consuela said sternly before he could get out. "You know you are sick with the diabetes. Why do you do all these bad things to yourself?" Then she said what I feared. "If we can't take care of you here, I tell the county and they put you in a stricter place." She wagged a finger at him.

That got his attention. Nick waved his hand for her to come closer as he eased himself out of the van and stood on the driveway. Still unsteady, he rocked a little. "Consuela, if I could get on my knees and beg, I would. I don't want to be anywhere but right here. No more messing around, and by the way that was all because of my wild brother there. He's the one who sought out the bordellos, the bars and the bimbos. Back to Bismarck with the bum." He smiled coyly.

Consuela did not look impressed with his alliteration. He made more promises. "From here on in, there'll be no more riotous living. I am on a *new* path." He stretched out the *new*.

"I'll be a good boy, I will, I promise. Right, bro?" He dragged me into the battle for the heart and mind of Consuela. I nodded.

"Okay, Nick. You come home now," said Consuela. I loved hearing those words from her. She let me give her a big hug. I should say, I let myself give her a big hug. Unbelievable, my recent transformation on that score. With José's help, Nick staggered into the house after greeting Barney and grabbing Arnie's cigarette for a drag.

The next day, Nick was good enough for a day out, maybe a little walking. He would need his strength—I had a message from Bonnie that a special night of revels had been scheduled for the following evening. In attendance: a family member of the foundation. Uncle Matthew.

Because he had lost weight in the hospital, Consuela had made a trip to the consignment store and found some shirts and pants and even a nice-looking pair of shoes. When I got there, he was waiting for me. He had on faded jeans and a long-sleeved Pendleton shirt. He looked put together—and glad to be back home.

"Where we going, bro?"

Frieda had packed us an enormous picnic lunch. Inside the cooler were chips and guacamole, chicken salad sandwiches, an assortment of veggies and fruits, and a couple of mammoth cookies.

We set off. Nick settled down in the passenger seat of the van and lit a cigarette.

"I'd like to run up to Fairfield," I said. "Maybe we can find some people who knew you when you still were a capitalist."

"When I had ready money, yes?"

"Yeah, when times were a little better than now."

I took his silence as affirmation.

132

the whole story
circuitous

"I thought we'd find out where you lived. Maybe the post office has undelivered mail. I don't know."

"Fairfield, eh? How the hell did I get up there? Damn near halfway to Sacramento." Nick might have been homeless in Fairfield before hitting Haight Street. He may have been booted out of the city after time on the street there.

"I want to find where you unloaded the Audi and your bass fiddle. The last things that helped you pay the rent for a while, buy groceries." He yawned. "Maybe we can talk to your landlord. Maybe he's saved something from when you were living there. What do you think?"

"Oh, I think I'll take a little nap here before we hit the hot spots of my former life." He flicked the cigarette out the window and laid his head back against the headrest. He never brought up Big Sur. He had either forgotten my promise to go there or he found the idea of Fairfield intriguing. He slept the rest of the way and woke up when I stopped to ask somebody where the Fairfield post office was.

My source was a guy on the street who looked like he was about our age. "It's a very small building you'd never guess is the post office. Straight ahead until you see a line of people stretching into the street and all looking madder than hell. That's the post office. Good luck."

"Look for the world's smallest post office," Nick said, condensing the directions.

"About the size of a stamp," I volleyed.

Nick lit a cigarette. "You say I lived here?"

"That's what a social worker said. You moved here three years ago. You had retired from the V.A. and were living on social security and a small pension."

"Probably pissed it away on riotous living."

"Life was good—right? You had a pretty decent apartment, rent was not too high. And you had your Audi."

"Gas hog and temperamental, a mechanic's dream. But a great old car back in the day."

We stepped out into a bright midday sun and took our

133

place in line. Half an hour later we were next for service at the counter. The clerk took a look and seemed to grow suspicious at the sight of us. Accompanying Nick, I was becoming aware of how rapidly people gauged social status from the too-large coat or the patched and frayed sweater or the mismatched shirt and pants.

"Can I help you two?"

"I'm having my mail held for me." Nick could always tell a convincing lie.

"Name and address," answered the clerk dismissively. That shut Nick up.

I gave the clerk an envelope on which I'd written Nick's name and my guess at the last month he had lived there. "My brother here used to live in Fairfield until a couple of years ago. I'm trying to find out where, since he is having a little trouble remembering. Here's his full name. Can you check to see if you have any mail for him, something in a dead letter file? You know what I mean?"

"We would be obliged," said Nick.

"We don't hold mail that long. Did you give us a forwarding address or just move out?" His last words cubbyholed us — as if we had done something irresponsible, criminal even.

"He just moved out."

"We probably shredded it or returned the first-class mail to the sender. I'll look, but I bet we don't have a thing." He took the piece of paper and wandered off into the interior. A few minutes later he returned, carrying a beat-up ten-by-twelve manila folder.

"This should have been tossed out at least a year ago. It got caught between the pile going to the dumpster and a sorting table, must have slipped under the table. You're in luck, buddy." I could have kissed this guy with a green visor and a plastic pocket penholder — right out of a Norman Rockwell painting.

"Thanks, sir. I am very appreciative," said Nick.

"Can I see some ID?"

There was some shuffling and stomping in the line behind

us. Damn. I should have thought of that. Nick wasn't carrying anything more than a pack of cigarettes, and I didn't know what he had back at Sunnyslope. Consuela probably had all his records. Why the hell hadn't I figured on this?

"Sir, my brother had been homeless for a year after he left Fairfield. He doesn't have any ID on him. But I've got a letter from the San Mateo County Human Services that has his name and current address."

"Let me see it," said the clerk. I took the letter out of my billfold. Thank god I'd left it there. The form included the Sunnyslope address and phone number.

"And here's my drivers license. Same last name. I live in North Dakota."

"You got a bathroom here?" asked Nick. I held my breath.

"No, but you can use the one at the McDonald's across the street."

"Aha. They have one at the McDonald's on Stanyan Street, too. Good people." That earned a scowl from the clerk.

I had to wrap this up. I didn't want Nick wetting his pants, or worse. "Nick, squeeze. Just give me a minute." I prayed he was wearing diapers under the jeans. The clerk was already on the phone: Consuela must have answered. He was firing all kinds of questions at her. I could imagine her getting really confused.

The package was lying on the counter. I could see Nick's old address in Fairfield. I memorized it. We were in luck even if he wouldn't give us the bulky folder.

"Well, it all sounds okay," the clerk snorted. "Let me talk to my supe." When he left the counter again, there was a group gasp of exasperation behind us.

"Patience, citizens," said Nick, turning to the line as if about to pontificate. "The document on the counter contains anthrax spores. They start agitating when people get hostile. Stay calm and don't breathe deeply or you'll suck in those spores and die standing right where you are. Like the citizens of Pompeii when the lava lapped them up."

The people at the front of the line backed away a little and somebody shouted, "Call the cops!" There was swearing and a few threats. Just then the clerk returned with the supe, who heard the shouts and yelled at the crowd to shut up.

"The old guy says there's anthrax in the folder," somebody yelled.

"Baloney," said the supe. "All that's in there is dust. The folder's been here at least two years. We'd all have been dead months ago. The gentleman, he's mistaken." He picked up the folder and shook it over his head. Some people ducked.

"Here," said the supe. "Take this off our hands. Glad we could accommodate you folks."

"Thank you, sir," Nick responded. "Sure wish you had a bathroom." The clerk looked over our heads at the next person in line. Mission accomplished.

We turned and made our way past the line. Nick saluted as we walked out the door. Some people were still holding their breath and pinching their noses. Nick shook the parcel as if activating the anthrax.

He made it to the McDonald's across the street. Back in the van, he announced he was ready for Frieda's delicacies. We drove further into downtown and found a park with picnic tables where we could eat lunch. We consumed everything in the cooler.

Then we began to sort through two-year-old mail. I expected the worst when the first one I opened said, "Final notice." Other letters used different words but they all amounted to the same: a notice of eviction, threats to disconnect telephones, orders to appear in court.

"You were popular with the bill-collecting crowd, Nick."

"Fucking vultures," he muttered.

I was stumped. With Nick's crowing about sexual prowess as the cornerstone of his business plan, I expected at least a couple of lawyers' letters alleging sexual abuse of a female client. But nothing.

What happened next left me dazed. In the middle of the

1997

stack was a greeting-card-size envelope. The return address was his place on the Great Highway off Ocean Beach. The postmark was 1995. It was two years old. Maybe an earlier letter had been returned to the sender, who'd then sent a new envelope. The post office had the Fairfield address but by the time it arrived, Nick had disappeared. So had the letter.

My Ocean Beach search along the Great Highway for Land's End Aloft had been a failure, off by perhaps a few blocks. Now I had the address. I could find the apartment if I needed to.

I wanted to open this envelope. Right there. But I didn't want Nick to be present. Maybe it was just a greeting card on his birthday from former co-workers at California Veteran Services. But maybe it was a letter from a patient, or a friend in San Francisco. Clearly the postmark was much too late to be from my wife. If it were personal, then the writer would have known of Nick's disintegrating predicament as he fended off creditors and lost his property. I wanted the letter to capture the moment as his life skidded downward and he hit bottom and fell into the underground of homelessness.

The unknown sender would still be around. A witness to one of his late night rants who might remember something Nick had said about his late sister-in-law. Jeanne Marie.

"Fan mail?" he asked, eyeing the envelope.

"Yeah, right. Let's save it for when we return home."

Nick was growing agitated. "Let's be off, bro. Our chariot awaits us." He had already forgotten about the mystery letter.

I stashed everything back in the manila folder, including the envelope. I put the folder under my arm and we left the park.

This was no Big Sur excursion. We weren't touring the rugged coastal beauty along Highway 1 with waves washing up on rocky shores far below. No Hearst's Mansion. No quaint towns or sail-flecked harbors.

This trip was to the end of the road, where the money dried up, where possessions were sold off or repossessed, where he spent his last night sleeping in his own bed, where Nick started putting one foot in front of the other on the road of homelessness. —> enough —

We parked outside an apartment complex near the downtown district. It was a two-and-a-half story walkup building with fake bricks and a mansard roof straight out of the 1960s. The neighborhood looked poised to go to seed, filled with scraggly yards, trashy streets, one or two rusting automobiles on blocks in driveways. I pushed the button next to the name of the manager. My heart was racing.

"Relax, brother. We're not committing a crime."

"Can I help you?" The irritable male voice registered as suspicious.

"Hi. Yes, maybe. I'm here with my brother who used to be a tenant in your building."

"Okay. What do you want?"

"Well, he's now in a board and care home and seems to have lost his short-term memory. I'm trying to help him remember his life here. Can we talk to you?"

"When did he leave here?"

"About two years ago."

"What's his name?"

Nick broke in. "I'm Doctor Nick...." He was interrupted by a very loud sigh on the other end and the phone went dead.

"You remember him," I said to the dead phone. Either the guy was going to ignore us or he was on his way to the front door. Hard to tell. In a minute, the door opened and there he stood, a man maybe ten years younger than we were. He had a weary, collapsed look: sunken chest, sloping shoulders, wobbly jowls. But he didn't seem unfriendly.

"My name's Floyd," he said as he opened the door. "Long time no see, Doctor Nick." Nick was silent. I introduced myself. No handshakes. Floyd led us down a few steps to his office on the garden level. There were two chairs for guests. We sat opposite Floyd.

"So, Nick. You remember me?"

"Can't say I do, although your voice sounds familiar. Were you a vet I counseled at the V.A.?"

"No. I was the apartment manager when you lived here. You were in Unit 108. We had our ups and downs, you and I. How you doing these days?"

"Capital," said Nick. "And yourself?"

"Good days and bad days," said Floyd. He seemed to think in opposites, up and down, good and bad. He probably divided his tenants into saints and sinners. No question about Nick's camp.

"Nick is aware he made some bad choices, so you don't have to sugar coat what happened," I said. "Can you tell us about his time here? Does he owe you money?"

Floyd leaned back in his office chair and took a couple of deep breaths. His mouth twisted. Nick leaned forward, his chin resting on his hand.

"Well, Nick was a good tenant when he first moved in here. He paid his rent, got along with the other tenants, kept his place up. But gradually I got complaints, you know. Shouting over the phone, empty beer bottles thrown outside, loud music. He'd be gone over the weekend so people cut him a little slack. He said he was appearing at nightclubs down on Half Moon Bay. He said he was a doctor. Some days he behaved like one. Other days he behaved more like a patient. A mental patient, you know?" He sighed.

I grimaced. Nick stared at Floyd.

"Some women tenants were after me to get rid of you." He looked straight at Nick. "You were a little *too* friendly." He turned to me. "Inappropriate, you know? It got real tense. He got to be more of a problem tenant than I could...well, he was driving me nuts. "

"And then?" I dreaded the answer.

Floyd sighed again. "I'd talk to him and then he'd shape up for a while, but then he was back to being a nuisance. Model tenant one day, pain in the ass the next. Then late with rent, until finally he quit paying altogether. Kept telling me he was going up to Sacramento to have the V.A. raise his pension, telling me some big investments he made were about to pay off. After he failed to pay three months running, I had to start eviction proceedings. It got ugly."

He stopped and faced Nick. "I liked you, Nick. When you were sober, you were fun. Great sense of humor. When you had too much to drink or when you were smoking dope, you made life miserable for all of us. You were so damn argumentative. You were always right, everybody else was wrong. Fun or misery, boom or bust. That sums it up."

"I appreciate your frankness. And you finally evicted him, when?"

"It was after he had to pawn his bass fiddle. The rest of us were glad to see it go. I told him about my friend who ran a pawnshop in town, said he'd be happy to buy it. I gave Nick a ride there. His Audi had stopped running and he had sold it for junk. I helped on that too. I had a friend who bought and sold used cars. He bought it, although we had to pay to have it towed to the lot. So, without a car, Doctor Nick stopped being away weekends. Seven days a week of loud music, late nights. Quiet days, loud nights. Then those three months of nonpayment—that's when I evicted him."

He looked at Nick again. "Don't know if you remember, but I gave you your deposit money back. I shouldn't have, maybe, but you needed the money, and I've got a heart, you know."

I reached toward my pocket. "I'd be glad..."

Floyd stopped me. "No, don't do that. I don't regret it, really."

"Thanks. Say, your two friends, the pawnshop owner and the car salesman, they still around?"

"You bet. Chet's Pawnshop. The car guy's name is Carlisle.

Name fits like a glove, right? Car-lisle. I'll give you directions." He started scribbling on a notepad and passed me the sheet when he was done. He stood up. So did I.

Nick stayed seated, and quietly, almost apologetically, asked, "Any friends? Visitors?"

Floyd scratched his head and looked at Nick. "Uh, not that I remember. There was a lawyer who came by once or twice. He gave me his card. I don't have it anymore. Friends? No, can't say I remember any."

My throat got tight. He couldn't remember any friends. I hoped the mystery envelope would yield a friend. "Thanks for your time," I said.

Nick had sat there pondering all this, stroking his chin. "I don't sound like I was a good tenant, mister...."

"Floyd. Like I said, not at the end. Beginning okay. End not so."

"Floyd, since then I've been sober—with just a couple of slips. I know it doesn't change what happened, but I'm sorry." He stood up.

For a change, I didn't feel as if I needed to apologize for Nick. Floyd led us out the front door and pointed in both directions. "You can get to the pawn shop either this way or that way. Left or right, makes no difference. Road actually runs in a circle. Bye, Nick. Good luck."

Nick said nothing, but saluted the man he didn't recognize.

En route to the pawnshop, I asked Nick, "You okay with this?"

"I'm along for the ride, bro. I couldn't tell you what comes next." He touched my arm. "Why are you doing this? Why are we visiting *terra* something or other?"

"*Terra incognita.*"

"Right. Why? Ben—you're not making amends, are you?"

141

He gave me a half smile. That was the first time he had said my name since I'd arrived. Otherwise it was "bro" or "brother." And he had linked my name to the twelve-step program that he loved to mock. But he was responding. He was thinking in real time. And why shouldn't he ask why?

"Or are you doing your duty? You were always the dutiful son. Now the dutiful brother."

I wanted to push him out of the car. I hated how he mocked me for being the good son and brother. What I valued in myself translated for Nick into imperious asshole.

"To quote Floyd back there, you were driving me crazy." I made myself take a breath. "But I let you down, when you probably needed me the most."

"The court rules that amends are duly noted. You've done your duty."

"Damn you! I'm not doing it out of duty! I'm doing it for me, and I have retained about this much love for you, you know?" I pinched my thumb and forefinger together.

"I'll take it," he said quietly.

I believe I felt a tiny endorphin rush.

We found Chet's Pawnshop. It smelled like old leather. So did the proprietor, who was grey-mustachioed and somewhere in his sixties.

"You brought in a bass fiddle a couple of years ago? Is that right?" I had explained the situation to him but he directed the question at Nick. "I'm trying to remember you coming in with your fiddle. I would have remembered that."

Nick was getting ornery. "I would have been a mean sonofabitch. It would have been like cutting off an arm. I can't believe I handed over Excalibur. I probably didn't get what it was worth, Chet, right? Did you cheat ol' Nick?"

"I don't think so."

That made me laugh.

Chet stood and reached behind him for a notebook. "I had an assistant who filled in for me once a week back then. It could have been one of those days." He was paging through a notebook. "Aha. 'Bass fiddle.' I have a date. September 21, 1995. My assistant stored a bass fiddle in the rear of the shop, where we have more humidity. Let me go look."

He left us there. Nick started to sweat. He patted himself with a handkerchief. "Come *on*, Chet," he whispered. He tapped the desk with his fingers in keeping with the pendulum of a grandfather clock in the corner.

"Here you are, folks," shouted Chet, still hidden in a corridor on the other side of a vast mound of stuff that looked like it hadn't been inventoried in years. He appeared, carrying a sorry-looking bass fiddle. It had splotches of discoloration and some rough chip marks. A couple of strings were broken. No wonder it was still safe and sound.

"Excalibur, you old son of a bitch." Nick's eyes widened. "I'd like to hold it before we go."

"Records show we paid you one-hundred for it."

I pulled out my checkbook and started writing. "I'll buy it back. Same price."

"Hey, I'm sure it's worth more than that." The man laid a hand on my forearm, and the pen stopped.

"Well if it is," I countered, "it'd take a lot more than that to bring it up to what it's worth." I completed the check, handed it to him and picked up the fiddle. Nick brushed some dust off the wood.

"Where's the bow?" asked Nick.

Chet laughed at that. "Let me find it." Back he went, and minutes later he returned. "That'll be another twenty-five."

"Bull-fucking shit it will be, Chet," announced Nick. "You bought both for $100." Nick's mean streak intimidated Chet and he handed over the bow. We said thanks and loped off to the van. I carried the fiddle, Nick the bow. The trip was worth it now.

"Chet the cheat," declared Nick as we drove away.

"That's how he makes his living, right? Nice guys don't last in that business."

After Chet, I was ready to quit treating stops on this

odyssey like the Circles of the Inferno or the Stations of the Cross. They were just the last appointments in Nick's calendar, before he didn't need a calendar.

I said we'd find the used car lot now. Nick reached over and grabbed my arm. "You heard Floyd. I sold it for parts. There's nothing to find. But, Ben? Thanks."

"You sure?" I asked.

"Yup."

"Okay, then tell me an Audi story."

"Sure. Lots of times, when the sun was coming up over the ocean, I'd settle down for a nap after a long night of music making down by Half Moon Bay. Excalibur was in the front seat and I was in the back. Life was good."

He sounded happy in the remembering. I could tell he was thinking of it as a dreadful loss. I couldn't stop thinking—we die by degrees. If we are mindful only of each downward step and not the bottom step, dying could be pretty damn hilarious.

As we approached the freeway on the way back, Nick poked my arm. "You've turned up a tight-assed apartment manager and a scurvy pawn shop operator. Not one dazzling dame."

"I'll bet you were celibate, Nick. Poverty is linked to chastity in our religion, remember?"

He looked at me wide-eyed.

"I'm joking. I'm sure you were your usual studly self."

He leaned his head back against the headrest. "Wait. I remember something I'll never forget. If you head for Sacramento, I'll show it to you."

It was maybe three in the afternoon. We were approaching Interstate 80. It would be a long drive back at night if we went the other way to Sacramento. But if he recalled one episode, a single something that happened in the last two years, why the hell not take a little longer? Maybe something momentous was just around the corner in Sacramento.

"All right! Sacramento, here we come!" Keep the conversation going. "How about that Floyd guy?" I laughed. "Good and bad, right and wrong, ups and downs."

"Noble and ignoble," he parlayed.

"The responsible brother," I said.

"The brother profligate," he replied.

"The good brother." I pointed to myself. "In favor."

"The bad brother." He pointed to himself. "Out of favor."

"The prodigal. The dutiful." I pointed from him to me.

"Action and reaction." He stopped and looked at me. "We created each other. There was an I, so there had to be a you."

"Do you think so?" I hadn't heard this idea from him before. I looked over at him, but nothing more.

We arrived in Sacramento an hour later. "What are we looking for?" I asked him. He had been quiet after our banter, just smoking and gazing out the window.

"Ask somebody for the tent city for the homeless."

I wanted to ask why, but didn't. There was a cop on the corner a block ahead. We rolled to a stop, and I lowered the window and asked directions. The cop looked us over and described how to get there.

"Not the part of Sacramento we want visitors hanging around," he said. "Why you want to go there?"

"Looking for a long-lost love," Nick answered. The cop did not seem amused or empathetic. I thanked him for the directions. When we pulled away, I repeated the cop's question.

"This place is somewhere I remember clearly. Surprised?"

I nodded yes.

"I remember taking a bus one day to Sacramento. I think it was just before Christmas, you know, outdoor decorations, Christmas trees in all the windows. I was lonesome and really broke. I went to the V.A. and asked for help. All I got was a little emergency cash. I blew most of it that day on beer and didn't even have enough to catch a bus back to Fairfield. And so I spent the night at this tent city for the homeless."

After a couple of wrong turns, we found the place. It was near a river. A motley collection of tents had been set up haphazardly across a field. The tents were in all shapes and sizes, some old, some new, some for six people, others for singles. I thought about Floyd the dualist back at the apartment: some fine-looking tents, some rotten-looking. The scene was like one of Brueghel's helter-skelter village squares. We got out of the van and started walking into the thick of it.

"I walked in here bombed out of my head," Nick mused. "I wandered around for a while. There must have been a couple hundred people. Cops and social workers were crawling all over the place."

As we walked, I saw the same cast of characters, maybe even the very persons Nick had encountered, the same homeless people lined up for food, the same police officers checking for liquor or drugs or weapons, and the same eager staff and volunteers serving meals and accepting donations of food and clothing from passersby.

"I spent the night with a woman in her tent." He chuckled. "Funny how I remember this. I had been just howling at the moon and circling around from one tent to the next."

"No room in anybody's inn," I said.

"I had passed her a couple of times. She was sitting by a fire with the biggest goddamn dog I'd ever seen.

"'If you're looking for a bed, you can sleep in my tent,' she finally yelled out after about my fiftieth time around. She was no spring chicken, about my age. Well, she invited me in and offered me a big old bedroll. 'Boy oh boy,' I thought. She plopped down on one side of the tent, and right alongside her in the middle is that big goddamn dog. Never left her side. I crawled very quietly into the bedroll next to the mastiff. Its teeth were as big as walrus tusks. She said, 'No booze, no sex, and no groping unless you care to lose your hand.'"

I didn't interrupt. This was momentous.

"The next morning when I woke up, she had made coffee and was toasting some bagels over a fire. Then she sent me on my way with a couple of bucks for the bus ride. Said she was going to church somewhere. I thanked her and would have hugged her, but the hound of hell made me back off.

"Saved my life that night. I remember somebody telling us how low the temperature got. It was about 30 degrees."

"Remember her name?"

"Carol. I remember volunteers singing Christmas Carols that morning. I called her my Christmas Carol."

"Can I help you gentlemen?" A cheerful young blonde-haired woman approached us. She was wearing an apron, an Oakland Angels sweatshirt and a pair of jeans. "You're new here, yes?"

"Actually, no. I spent an evening here a couple of years ago," Nick replied. "Delightful amenities."

"Chili on the menu tonight. Please join us." She pointed to the nearby line of men, women and children.

"Actually I'm looking for someone named Carol." Nick stood close to the woman. "An old friend."

She backed up a step. "Carol. Oh, yes, of course. Carol and her beautiful dog. Um, Benny."

At first I thought I was wearing a nametag. Then I realized she was referring to Carol's dog. I laughed politely. She looked puzzled.

"That's my name."

"I remember his teeth more than anything," Nick said.

"I'm so sorry. Carol died several months ago. She gave the dog to a friend."

Nick looked away for a moment, kicked the dirt and made the sign of the cross on himself.

The woman squeezed Nick's arm and guided the two of us into the line. She stood next to us. "Carol had many high school students befriend her in her sickness. She was lucky."

"Yes she was," replied Nick. A volunteer gave us trays, and

then another handed us bowls of steaming chili, salad, bread and cookies. We sat down at a long table and ate silently. Conversation among the other diners was soft, almost monastic.

Then Nick broke the grand silence with an announcement. "About Benny, Carol's dog." Some looked up from their chili, others kept on slurping it in. "Great name for a watchdog, don't you think? My brother here is named Ben."

Some embarrassed laughter. One man, about our age, looked me up and down. "I'd say the dog was better looking." The grand silence dissolved into puddles of mirth. I grinned, trying to look stupid, as if I was offended. The volunteer who had invited us to eat looked over from the serving table and smiled. Still laughing, the guy who made the comparison came over and slapped me on the back. Nick looked slightly irritated. *He* was the comedian here, right?

After the meal, Nick and I said goodbye to everyone and we walked over to where the volunteer with the Oakland A's sweatshirt was chatting with other diners. Nick squeezed the volunteer's hand. "Carol gave me a new challenge in life: survive the night. And I did, every night, until I almost didn't. Brother Ben here's from North Dakota. He's *my* watchdog."

She looked at me with a smile so appealing I thought she might be Bonnie's sister. "I can assure you, Ben, you are much better looking than Carol's dog."

I laughed, said thanks, reached into my pocket and gave her a twenty. "In memory of Carol," I said.

We were back in the van. He grabbed my hand and held it to his heart. "I bet she had quite a funeral celebration, that Carol. I wish I'd been there. I wish I'd known. Amazing lady."

He fell asleep as soon as we left Sacramento. I savored my initiation into the ranks of the homeless. It seemed an easy step, from my life to theirs. This day was as memorable for me as it was for Nick. I promised myself I'd call Frances and Clare that night.

Back at Sunnyslope, Nick set out for the front door and its two raggedy doormen who surely had a spare cigarette or two between them. I stopped him, hugged him and said, "See you tomorrow. For the revels, okay?" I said goodnight to José who'd opened the front door to let Nick in.

Back at the B&B, I made a conference call to my daughters. I told them the tent story. Usually quick to hypothesize what every step with Nick meant, they listened quietly. I told them about the "revels" but not about the letter. I promised to call them each again soon.

I sat in semi-darkness in my room and fished in the manila folder for the letter. I retrieved the envelope and opened it. My hands were shaking. I knew this was a terrible violation, but I couldn't help myself. I had a feeling about it, and I had to know. There was another, smaller envelope inside the outer envelope. A note was pinned to it: "Dear Nick, I'm a tenant living in an apartment on the Great Highway. I was cleaning a closet the other day when I found this letter addressed to you at my address. I figured you used to live here. I called the post office and they gave me an address for someone with your name in Fairfield. Hope this reaches you. The letter had been opened. I didn't read it."

I pulled off the paper clip that held the note. The postmark on the inside envelope said Bismarck, North Dakota. The year was 1991. I recognized the stationery. The handwriting. They were my wife's.

good build up — I realized & hooked here.

I woke late. Bonnie and Joyce had left written messages at the B&B. I found them on the table in the breakfast room.

Bonnie's was on foundation letterhead. "The proposal has been submitted to the foundation: $50,000 for a planning grant, to be followed by full submission the following year. The grant application process includes a site visit. Tonight, at the revels. The board will want to meet the brother—you. Excited? We're halfway there, Ben." Under her name it read, "President."

Joyce's was really — true to style — a commentary. "Homelessness is nothing new in San Francisco, but the drama of Nick's arc of recovery will captivate Bonnie's board of directors. Your brother has gone from street derelict to visionary starting a revolutionary new program for the mental health of nursing home residents. No question, this city is the capital of self-reinvention. Can't wait to find out how Fairfield went. Joyce."

I brought the bass fiddle to the musician who provided the band for the Elder Town revels. He said he could "gussy it up," put some new strings on it and have it ready for me in an hour. I wandered down the street and bought two San Francisco Giants baseball caps. Back at the B&B, I called Nick. Consuela said he was napping, as he often did on the day of the revels. She said she'd have him down at Elder Town in plenty of time.

Bonnie picked me up at eight-thirty. A designer skirt and a peach-colored jacket gave her a very professional look. This was Bonnie's show all right. She and Andrea had spent hours putting together the program.

"You're going to love it, Ben. Andrea has been unbelievable. By the way, Joyce has a special role tonight. It's a surprise."

"Bonnie, have you ever heard of a tent city in Sacramento?" I remembered she had run a school system there. I guessed she might have had something to do with encouraging students to volunteer at the tent city.

"Of course. I used to volunteer there. Why?"

I looked out the window as dusk fell. Could she have served Nick soup there? I told her of yesterday's side trip to Sacramento and Nick's night in a tent just before Christmas a couple of years ago. I said a homeless woman named Carol put him up for the night, next to her big dog, a mastiff that ensured Nick's temporary erectile dysfunction.

Bonnie laughed and shook her head. "Of course I knew Carol. Everyone knew Carol. A great lady. Small world, Ben, isn't it?"

I told her that Carol had died not very long ago, and was

150

cared for by a group of high school students as she was dying. Bonnie nodded.

Outside Elder Town, we sat in the car after she had turned off the ignition. I told her about Fairfield, about Floyd and Chet. But not about the post office, not about the letter. While we chatted, vans were dropping off the guests, most of them walking unaided or with walkers. Some were in wheelchairs. Aides accompanied many. It was a night on the town in Elder Town. It was exciting.

I took a deep breath. Bonnie leaned across the coffee cup holder and squeezed my arm. "Don't worry, Ben. It's a lark. It'll be terrific."

She must have developed this thing about a lark in the convent. Things can't go wrong in a lark because there is no objective we are obliged to meet. It's a world without agenda. We just let go of the outcome and enjoy the moment. Stuff happens, yes? Okay, Bonnie. I'm in. I'll try. Life is a lark. Tonight at least.

We left the car just as a distinguished-looking guy a little older than I approached the entrance to Elder Town. He turned and saw Bonnie and waited for us. Bonnie introduced me to him after giving him a hug. "Meet Uncle Matthew." He shook my hand vigorously. I was balancing the fiddle in my left hand while I shook his hand. He was a little taller than me, a full, ruddy face, prominent teeth, a big smile, and an obvious wig.

"The family is very happy to meet you," said the man. He left no doubt *he* was the family. "Bonnie here has spoken so approvingly of what your brother has accomplished. We can't wait to meet him." He smiled confidently. "We" indeed.

"You are his only sibling, correct?" Uncle Matthew asked. I nodded. He looked me in the eye. "What do you think of this night revel idea?"

"Well, sir, of course I'm prejudiced," I said. "I think he's on to something."

"I do hope so," he replied. "We think it could be invaluable to elders in our many Catholic nursing homes."

I thought, wow, this is pretty easy, this fundraising.

"We'll find out the truth tonight. Carry on," he grunted.

"Yes sir." I actually saluted him. He smiled.

"I can't stay too long," he went on after a short breath. "It's late and I'll want to get back to the city."

The door to Elder Town opened and Andrea bounced, yes, bounced down the handicap ramp as if it were a sloping trampoline. "Welcome to the revels of the night!" She was beaming. The uncle looked her up and down, and seemed perturbed by her buoyancy. She took his hands. "So happy to meet you! We're all ready for you. Please come in."

I checked my watch. It was nine o'clock. Let the revels begin. And let my brother behave.

This was not the Elder Town I'd been introduced to just a few days ago. It had blossomed into something resembling one of Madonna's concert tour stages. Banks of sundown-banishing floodlights had been placed around the perimeter. Vases of fresh flowers had been arranged on stands among the lights. A huge disco ball hung over the room like an indoor sun ready to rotate on its orbit across the ceiling. The scent of mild incense wafted in the air.

There were about fifteen to twenty people besides the staff. The women looked to be dressed in their best outfits, mix-and-match styles and colors, lots of pink and pastel, some in slacks and blouses, others dressed for late formal evenings long departed from their social calendars. I counted four men. They too were looking sharp in their shiny slacks and sport jackets over polo shirts. The shirts endorsed everything from Tommy Bahama to the San Francisco Giants. There were three guys in semi-formal wear—the musicians. They quietly took the fiddle

Excalibur from me and hid it behind some equipment on the stage.

At the center of a circle of elders, a middle-aged woman dressed in yoga pants and a loose-fitting tank shirt was speaking softly, soothingly, about proper breathing. They all had their eyes shut. Their postures were as close to straight as they could get. They were making whooshing sounds, like wind in the forest. Every once in a while, someone coughed or sneezed. I thought of Esalen back in the day. "Whoosh. Whoosh." This was like an Elder Esalen.

On some mysterious cue, everyone stopped whooshing and opened their eyes. Within seconds, they started chatting excitedly and the volume increased. Suddenly, the rear door to the room opened. In bounded a pack of barking dogs accompanied by their shouting attendants. The San Francisco Animal Humane Society had brought along critters of all sizes, pedigrees and colors, enough to match up a canine with every elder.

The guy who had popped off about his rousing sex life on my first visit was wearing a Giants t-shirt tonight. He had let out the leash on a mid-size mutt that looked half whippet and half black lab. The mutt went right for Bonnie's uncle, who stood his ground and grimaced as the dog jumped on him and started sniffing around his crotch.

"Hello, friend, Aviva won't hurt you," yelled the would-be dog whisperer. He let the leash out enough so Aviva could continue her sniffing. "She's a hell of a dog, just a little nervous." Bonnie, who had been staying back, approached, petted Aviva and detached her from her uncle's slacks.

As if to explain Aviva's attack, the old guy said, "'Aviva' is Hebrew for 'springtime.' Blood runs fast when we're young! Hah!"

There followed thirty minutes of merry mayhem with elders grooming, snuggling and giving futile commands to the animals. Then Andrea announced it was time for pizza or some dietary substitution. The humane society staff began hustling the animals out of the room. Terms of deep endearment followed the menagerie out the door.

Everyone seemed mellow. Nothing rowdy. Of course Nick the un-mellow wasn't part of the picture yet. I wondered where he was. I gestured to Bonnie. She came over.

"Nick's going to make a grand entrance in about a minute. Before we have supper, there's time for some Q and A with the guests." She looked across the room and then up to the heavens. Her forehead creased. She read my thoughts. "Come on, Nick, behave," she whispered.

Andrea plinked a few keys on the piano. The room grew quiet. She introduced Uncle Matthew as the representative of the foundation. She reminded the audience that they had already met Bonnie and me.

People applauded vigorously, if a little self-consciously. The foundation, in the persons of Uncle Matthew and Bonnie, was paying attention to their dwindling share of this universe and they were proudly drawing back the curtain. The uncle's presence at this event said something that touched them deeply. In the face of their enthusiasm, I clung to my old fear of impending embarrassment at Nick's hands, just as I had done at the cathedral days earlier.

After some housekeeping announcements, Andrea did a little drumroll on the piano. "And heeeeere's Nicky!" Out from the kitchen strode Nick, wearing slacks that were a blazing white-and-blue-striped affair. His jacket was buckskin, too long in the sleeves, replete with fringes that, like their wearer, had seen better days. His shirt was purple and a size too big. He wore cowboy boots and a cowboy hat. He shuffled along in his boots, as if they were too heavy a load for his weak legs. I remembered he had a thing for western dress earlier in life, when he was liberating himself in the 1960s from "society's petty norms," as he loved to say.

Andrea came to him with a handheld microphone and held it to his mouth. Nick took a few breaths.

"How's everybody tonight? This is as *good* as it *gets*, right?" He punched the "g's" so the mic would pop. Everyone clapped and cheered. "I welcome my brother here from North Dakota, and I especially *greet* the gentleman from the...."

"Just 'the foundation' is okay," Bonnie shouted.

"From the foundation," he said. "I invite him to dive right into the program. So let's kick some ass."

Andrea winced. Bonnie bit her lip. The uncle coughed. I wanted to run and hide. Bye-bye, fifty grand. He was being his usual lowlife schmuck-of-a-self. Actually, I should have been relieved. He could've easily led off with, "Let's get this mother-fucker off the ground."

His regular audience of revelers giggled and chuckled, as his choice of words was nothing new to them. Then Nick had the grace to pause. I suspected he had noticed Uncle Matthew's shock.

"I meant to say we feel passionately about sundowning, the name for the scourge of end-of-day anxiety. Dysfunctional behaviors run amuck across the country. The prescribed treatment is always more pharmaceuticals." Looking straight at Bonnie's uncle, he said, "You, the foundation, can be a pioneer by creating a new paradigm. I call it seniors taking back the night. Lovely Bonnie there, you have a question before we start eating?"

A rehearsed Q and A. "Nick, is it true that more than half of the residents who are in assisted-living facilities or nursing homes are basically alone? Their children and grandchildren are either too busy for them or live too far away."

"You said it, honey!" said a guest.

Bonnie continued. "And then there are the ones that end up on the streets, homeless."

"Surviving the night," Nick said in a half-whisper, and then, in a stronger voice, "We are written off as delusional and detrimental drags on society. Sometimes by those closest to us." He shot a direct look at me and then at Uncle Matthew.

A woman in a wheelchair pushed it forward. Long gray hair framed a lively face. She sat straight, an absolutely breathtakingly beautiful old woman with the aplomb of someone who has seen it all. I hadn't noticed her on the first visit. A bank of lights behind her silhouetted her wheelchair. She wore a beige jacket over a blue blouse and beige slacks.

She spoke with a strong clear voice. "Hello to our guests. My name is Laura. I was a therapist for 45 years. My patients ranged across all ages, educational backgrounds and emotional maturity levels. I've seen them all. I think my patients all suffered from a plague of isolation. Everywhere I looked. Isolation happens when there are no sustaining common bonds. No central commons, as it were, as you see in European cities."

Vigorous applause from the other guests rippled through the room. As if stunned by a sudden rifle report, the uncle sat up straight as she spoke.

"I think the next generation is terrified of loneliness or aloneness!" Her voice grew stronger, louder. "Television, computers, cell phones. And the new thing called the Internet. Got news for you, you young ones: when you're old, you're *alone*. No more toys."

She paused for effect. "We've replaced tools with toys. When's the last time you saw a teenager holding a saw or scythe or even a screwdriver? Now it's Walkmans or DVD players. Toys!"

I saw people's hands twitch, as if their fingers remembered wrangling hammers and wrenches or clutching serving spoons.

"What Doctor Nick has done with this revels of the night program is simply to validate us. We're old but we're not dead."

Cheers, whistles and applause.

She stopped to chuckle. "He sometimes gets carried away, ol' Nick. Oh, he's obsessed with *sex*, for instance…." She paused. There was laughter around the room. Her timing was dead on. A male guest rotated his hips suggestively, eliciting guffaws and tut-tuts.

She went on. "I think that's called compensation." Her tone of voice made it clear it was loving teasing, no more.

Nick mimicked writing her name down on a police blotter as the room echoed with laughter. The uncle started to laugh, but suppressed it. I watched his throat, the bulging arteries. Stop, lady, I thought, before he....

"Many, many therapists in San Francisco back in the day were hung up on sex. Some made a mess of things. Maybe Nick did. But that was then and this is now. Here's my point. He is taking us as we *are*—still sensual beings. Touch is all that remains to us. He has hit the sweet spot of aging with this nutty combination of nighttime programs. We are not as afraid of the night's loneliness as we once were. It works! Don't medicate us! Massage us! Loving touch opens us to whatever you want to call it: the spirit, the self, the soul." She looked intently at Bonnie's uncle. "Your support will make all the difference! Help us continue what we've started."

Clapping and whistling ensued. Uncle Matthew clapped with gusto. Had she made him a convert? And she had cleverly absolved Nick of any sins he might have committed in his professional life. More than I was willing to do. The weight of the Fairfield letter pressed down on my brain.

The woman took a deep breath—she clearly wasn't finished. "This night is about the power of nostalgia. There's no time like the night to remember the old days. Something happens in our brain when we talk about birthdays and holidays and graduations, about weddings and divorces, and births and deaths. Nostalgia is the best tonic in the world for aging! It connects us and our bodies to the past."

This time, guests hooted and stomped their feet. Andrea walked over to the woman and hugged her. Bonnie winked at me.

"No need to waste more time on testimonials," said Nick. "We're hungry, right?" All the men and a few women let out

[handwritten margin note: with me knew at this point)]

piercing whistles. "Time for questions as we eat. Dancing starts in a half-hour. Party on, elders!"

Nick walked slowly over to where Andrea, Bonnie and Uncle Matthew were standing. I edged closer. "Excuse my slip of the tongue, sir," he said to the uncle. "I'd like to invite you to join us in the dancing later."

"Oh, I might not be able to stay," said the uncle, but he kept staring at Laura.

"I insist." Nick wagged his finger at the uncle. "We are making history tonight! Ask me anything, as long it's not for some of my greatest dirty jokes." This was Nick, barely behaving.

The uncle shriveled a bit under Nick's onslaught, but then bloomed again as his eyes sought out and found Laura in her wheelchair. He was friendly but all business when he addressed Nick. "How will your program help Catholics? After all, that is our central mission."

For the first time, Nick looked bewildered. Bonnie came to his rescue.

"My uncle calls attention to the mission of the family foundation to make a difference in the lives of Catholics in the United States or of people in Catholic countries in the Americas."

"Ah, yes," said Nick. "I think my brother here may have something to contribute." He stared at me. I was being asked to witness to his appeal to Catholics. What appeal? My brother? The iconoclast, the free-love enthusiast?

"You see, he teaches Latin, and stays in touch with the Vatican on a regular basis." Nick spoke with an earnest flicker in his voice, as if he were sitting on a vibrator. "Brother, how do you see the revels of the night helping the pope's legions?"

I managed an authoritative smile as my mind went blank. Where was my stash of puffery? I started. "Nick's program deals in mysteries. As you know, the mysteries of baptism and new life are central to Catholic teaching. The liturgical celebration of baptism always takes place at night, at the Easter vigil. Candles, bells and incense, as you well know, stimulate the senses. *Ad fidem per sensum.* To faith through sensuality. The community listens to stories, sacred history. There's music, sacred dance, the ritual meal. They return home." I smiled at the uncle. "It's a kind of liturgical rebirth—a nostalgia trip, as Laura so beautifully put it." I smiled at the uncle.

Bonnie nodded a fervent *yes, yes.* "That is *so* true, Ben. It's amazing how close the analogy is." I suddenly knew what her uncle's next question would be.

And it came. "Where do you go to church while you're visiting?" he asked.

I was ready. "The cathedral." I shot Bonnie a wink.

"How about some pizza?" Bonnie hooked her arm through her uncle's.

"Why yes, I think I should stay for pizza and watch the dancing start." He was starting to loosen up. "After all, eating together is a highlight of the evening, isn't it?"

A lady reveler sashaying by with three slices of pizza on a paper plate overheard the "highlight" comment. "Oh no, dearie, it's the massage therapy that comes later. Oooh la la. Tingly all over." She bumped the uncle with her hip and sashayed away.

I was reminded that it wasn't just Nick who could torpedo this. As usual, I feared the worst. The uncle would convince the family to reject the proposal. Improve the lives of Catholics? The revels were more likely deleterious to Catholics—the suggestive behavior, the appeal to emotions, the push over the edge for the timid and weak. Would a Catholic institution stand for this kind of physicality?

"Is he married?" I whispered to Bonnie.

"A widower. Very lonely beneath the staunch Catholic surface."

I knew just who might bring him around.

The disco ball sprinkled tiny colored spangles across the room. Musicians appeared with sax, drums and guitar. And there at the piano sat Joyce, next to a microphone.

Ah, so this was the surprise. She wore a classy little black dress and waved at me. A shiver shot through me. It wasn't just the sexy black dress, it was her vitality. For me, sensuousness always trumped raw sexiness.

"Nostalgia rocks! Let's dance!" she cheerily announced. "Requests encouraged." And before anyone could shout out a song title, the band started playing "Shall We Dance?" from *The King and I*. To my surprise, everyone held back around the perimeter of that room. I saw why—Nick and Andrea were walking slowly to the center. She was supporting him by the arm. Nick smiled big, and grasped Andrea around the waist. They slowly, very slowly, revolved around the floor. He was the king of Siam—albeit in a fringed western jacket, waltzing with the beautiful English governess—well, a thoroughly modern woman in a miniskirt. After a minute or so, Andrea left Nick and went straight to Uncle Matthew, who was standing next to me. Without a word, she took his arm and led him out to the floor. Meanwhile, Bonnie slid into Nick's grasp and they danced in place.

Now there were dancers everywhere. Those in wheelchairs held hands with their attendants. Laura danced by herself, sending her wheelchair spinning, as if a turntable.

Aha. Uncle Matthew led Andrea directly into Laura's path and swerved away just as the music ended. He had made his move.

"We've had a request for the 'Pennsylvania Polka,'" Joyce announced into the mic.

Uncle Matthew approached Laura, and stood near her as she revolved her chair. How does one spin a wheelchair provocatively? Suddenly, she was Venus on a rotating half shell. Then, she stopped the chair, leaned forward and gripped his hands, and stood. Andrea looked at Bonnie and grinned like a proud mother of a shy son. This new couple stood in place, swaying despite the upbeat tempo.

Bonnie tapped me on the shoulder and I said, "What are the chances of your family agreeing to back this orgy? I'm betting on Laura being the trump card tonight!"

We worked our way toward Nick, who sat wiping his forehead and tapping a foot. Bonnie and I stopped in front of him.

Nick was looking directly at me. "Hey, bro, what do you think?"

"I think you are a rock star, brother," I said and tugged at a few of the cleaner fringes on his jacket.

Bonnie helped Nick up. "Let's just hop in place, sweetie," he grunted. "I'm preserving my energy for later."

Someone dimmed the lights and the disco ball seemed brighter. The mood was all romance, as if blood pressure cuffs and oxygen masks were the new corsages and braces.

An hour later, Joyce announced that the band would wrap up with a string of slow "hold-me-tight" numbers. "We've had requests to lower the heart rate," she said. The band played "Have I Told You Lately That I Love You?"

The outnumbered men were quickly snapped up. Laura kept a lock on Uncle Matthew, or was it the other way around? Hard to tell. The couples leaned into each other, women with men, women with women. In the light of day, they knew all the names and warts and ailments of their partners, but the darkened room made them all young and healthy, almost mythical. In this world, dementia was actually a benefit: a step closer to the past. You didn't have to recognize *anybody*. Nostalgia in its purest form: memories unrolling like player piano scrolls.

"Final call. We've had a request for 'Laura.' Find a partner," Joyce drawled in a velvety voice. "And Nick, come on up." The place ricocheted with whistles and clapping. Andrea led Nick, looking surprised but pleased, to the stage, where a stool had been placed next to the piano. Then Andrea walked over to me, took me by the arm and led me to the stage.

"Nick's brother has a present for him," she announced. I went over to get the fiddle and pressed it against Nick's chest. It was the first time I'd seen him moved to tears without the aid of beer or dope.

"This is Nick's old fiddle from back in the day," I announced. Like high school kids at a school dance, everyone crowded around the stage and cheered. "Like Nick, it's been around the block," shouted one of the guys.

"Laura," Joyce whispered to Nick, and the band began accompanying the two of them.

Bonnie took my hand, and we danced amid arthritic bodies moving in unison under the glitter of the disco ball. Uncle Matthew steered Laura through the crowd. Couples changed partners, and this scrum of elders became a spontaneous cotillion of elegant, graceful dancers. Faces flickered past me like an old movie film.

And then the music stopped. After a round of cheers for his performance, Nick shouted into a mic, "Bedtime!" Holding a lit candle, he led a procession of elders out of the activity hall and into a room illuminated by floor lamps dotting cots. People disappeared into the large restrooms and returned wearing pajamas or gowns.

In the procession to the dorm room, Uncle Matthew was pushing Laura's chair, making an end run for two cots that were separated by only a few feet.

"Let me remind everyone," shouted Andrea. "No moving cots. If you want to touch someone, it's from three feet away and nothing below the neck except toes or arms."

Bonnie had brought a pair of new pajamas for Uncle Matthew. "A gift I thought you might like," she said, opening a cover of the box. For the first time that night, I saw how charming he looked when he smiled. When her uncle returned, he lay down in an adjoining cot to Laura's and reached for her face. It was a chaste gesture, but loaded with desire.

The massage team entered the room. Andrea lowered the lights. "Okay, everyone, once again we welcome our friends from the San Francisco School of Massage."

I walked over to Nick. Except for our brief exchange, we hadn't spoken the whole evening. His forehead shone with sweat. He had taken off the Wild Bill Cody jacket and was unbuttoning his shirt. His eyes were red, misty.

I was at my apologetic best. I gripped his arm. "Hey, I want you to know I'm more than impressed. I'm a believer!" I kept thinking about the envelope in my pocket, but I tried to find my better self. There would be no resolution of my feelings until I read the letter. But I knew the right thing to do was acknowledge him apart from me—as someone capable of good in the bigger world.

He took my arm and spoke confidentially. "I'm trying to do important work out here. I know I can be a fuck up. I know who I am. But that's not all of me." An aide slipped a black caftan over his shoulders. He gathered it around him, like a cloak of power.

Extra cots had been set up for Bonnie and Joyce and me. Andrea brought gowns for the three of us and off we went to change. At the foot of every cot was a folder of medical records showing the elders' physical condition, ailments, tics and sensitivities. After consulting them, the therapists, one by one, sent soothing comments to their charges, like snowflakes gently blanketing the prairie. Skillful fingers rubbed necks and shoulders and arms, and feet and toes.

I gave myself over to the calm.

An hour later, a stout lady shouted from her cot, "Story time, Nick. Put us to sleep, you sly old daddy."

"Time for a bedtime story for all my lady loves and my

gentlemen pals?" Nick sat down heavily on a chair that had been placed on a small platform. He growled low into the mic, "Listen up, boys and girls. It's the story of that bad old field mouse, Frederick."

"What a ham!" Bonnie giggled and then clapped her hand over her mouth.

"So once upon a time, there were these field mice having the time of their lives. Summertime, and the living was easy. But at the end of summer the field mice stopped playing around and got serious. That was a big deal, because *these* field mice *loved* to party—like San Francisco in the 1970s."

"Yes!" shouted a couple of male elders. Several women made knowing sounds, "uh-huh," like they remembered some pretty wild parties, too.

"Well, the head field mouse assembled them all one morning and told them the party was over. 'Start gathering corn and nuts and straw for the winter,' he said. Now Frederick was a cool cat—a mellow mouse, pardon—a hipster who just lay there daydreaming and looking up into the blue sky while the other mice did all the heavy lifting. You can imagine how they all felt about our lazy boy Frederick. 'Whoa, Frederick. So what's with the sloth? Why don't you help us gather corn and nuts and straw for winter?'

"Well, our boy Frederick came right back at them. 'Hey, I *am* helping. Can't you see? I am gathering the sun's rays and storing up summer for winter. You just wait. You'll see.'

"Well, winter came, the snow fell, the wind blew, and the lakes and rivers froze. It was like North Dakota in January, right, bro?" Nick looked around until he found me. "And all the mice," he continued with a smile, "were ready to gang up on little Freddie. 'Okay, where's this great stuff you gathered? And how's it going to get us through this winter?'

"Well, Frederick stepped up. 'Close your eyes,' he commanded. They obeyed, and he conjured up summertime. With his words all the mice saw the sun's rays, and they felt warm all over. 'Keep 'em closed,' he said. 'See the colors of summer, the reds and blues and greens and yellows. And the smells of summer flowers! Roses and lilacs and lavender and jasmine!' All that beauty intoxicated them. They were drowsy, damn near drunk on dopamine, from the bounty of summer.

"Then the mice asked Freddy for the words of summer, and he told them a story about the powers of imagination. 'You can put yourself wherever you want to. If you are cold, or suffering, or in pain, think of the most beautiful place you've been in the world and imagine yourself there. And you will *be* there.' Like you've all heard ol' Doctor Nick say, *act as if*. Well, the field mice got it.

"And you know what they all shouted at their furry little comrade? 'You are a poet, Frederick!'"

Nick acknowledged the clapping and cheers. "So there's a moral, boys and girls, and *you* know what it is. We are all poets, right? When we're old, we can't lift the corn or gather the nuts or pack up the straw the way we used to. And maybe some of you—us—can't get it up any more," he cackled. "Right?" People shouted and grunted either affirming or denying what he said.

Nick went on. "What we can offer is the nonstop sun of nostalgia." He punched each syllable. "Summer memories can carry us through the winter. Beauty lasts because we have poetry and song and stories. And no matter what else we do, we can always tell our stories—of summer, of young love, of winter, of dark times. They are all stories of survival. Don't let your kids or your grandkids grow up without your stories, because it's our ultimate gift—remembering, surviving!'"

The total silence was his amen. He stood, extended an arm, and blessed his congregation. I alone knew Prospero was coming next, because for as long as I could remember, Nick fancied himself Shakespeare's great, aged character, who once wielded magical powers but now was reduced to ordinary human rank.

And it came. "To sum up, here's old Prospero: 'Now my charms are all o'erthrown and what strength I have's mine own, which is most faint. Gentle breath of yours my sails must

165

fill, or else my project fails, which was to please.'" He paused. "…and so forth."

From her cot next to my right, Joyce tapped my arm. "The poet laureate of Elder Town is saying goodbye."

I smiled, seeing that Nick's Prospero had evolved. He wasn't raging against sundown, against nightfall, against family. Tonight he was seeking spirits to enforce, art to enchant, and the breath of elders to fill the weakening sails of his earthly voyage. And it struck me: the Latin word *placebo* means "I will please." I now saw it: Nick's placebos were the fairy dust we all needed—know it or not. I'd spent most of my life in the "not" camp.

It was one in the morning. I fell asleep, joining my snoring, wheezing, coughing fellow revelers.

I woke up, with the rest of the room, when Andrea rang an old schoolroom bell at seven. Looking around, I was certain no one had died in the night.

Within twenty minutes most of the revelers were dressed and ready to leave. Nick stood at the door, hugging them one by one.

Uncle Matthew came along, pushing Laura in her wheelchair. "Ah, fast work," whispered Joyce.

"Bonnie, the foundation must fund this project," said Uncle Matthew firmly as he pushed the wheelchair toward us.

"Laura, your contributions have been invaluable," said Bonnie, adding a wink. "Thank you so much."

"Bonnie, don't leave for Quito without talking to me first," her uncle said. Bonnie smiled and hugged him.

Before we left, I called my B&B hosts, and asked if I could bring guests for breakfast. We drove straight there.

"Things came together, didn't they?" said Bonnie.

"Your smitten uncle will have the board lined up by the weekend," said Joyce.

Bonnie nodded but could hardly stifle a yawn. "Ben, tell Joyce about Sacramento."

I told Joyce the story of the lady named Christmas Carol and the Sacramento tent city, of Carol's invitation to Nick to spend the night with her—and her dog. We all laughed again.

Joyce nudged me. "I'm proud of you, Ben. That's a story for your grandkids."

Bonnie wiped her eyes with a tissue. "Here I go again," she sniffed.

We sat quietly. I felt this growing amazement at what Bonnie had accomplished in the last weeks. But I thought I sensed something restless in her, maybe the approaching end of this lark or the anticipation of the next lark on her schedule. Or some decision hanging over her. She was already foundation president. What now?

"Bonnie, do all your larks end up with you shedding tears for the suffering of others? Your future larks—will they all be as stressful as this one? What's next?"

Bonnie seemed surprised by the questions. "Well...."

"Tell him," said Joyce.

This might be interesting, I thought. The woman has something to say. She cleared her throat.

"You asked about whether I left the convent for somebody. Well, remember what I said about Notre Dame?"

"Sure. The late nights at the grotto. Priests and nuns discovering their sexuality. More action than on the football field. Scoring, Nick would call it."

"I made fun of it, but it was more serious than I let on."

"You met someone," I said. Half question, half guess.

"Yes. A priest. A future college president, no less." She laughed. "I first met him back in 1970. I had just made vows to my order of sisters. I went to Notre Dame to study theology before pursuing a degree in education. Well, he was there, too. We started a conversation after class one day, chatting about the new theology and the exciting young theologians on campus. And then we started going on late-night strolls, yes, to the grotto." She paused.

"We never went beyond kissing. He wasn't going to leave and neither was I. We stayed in touch through the years, letters, lunches when we were in the same city. So I told him six months ago I was leaving the sisterhood. And he wrote back and said...."

"'I'm leaving the priesthood!'" said Joyce, impersonating the priest. "The man has impeccable timing."

"His announcement hit the news," Bonnie said. "He's the president of a major Catholic college."

She smoothed the napkin lying by her plate. "He's interviewing for the presidency of a community college, here, in California. He'll be in San Francisco in two months. I don't know what will happen, but we both know where we'd like it to go."

"So the Stern Grove lark—why was this so important to you?" I wanted to know what drove this bright woman to forget about her future and get involved with Nick and me.

She smiled, her eyes bright. "A lark is a surprise fling just before the real thing. You know, out of the blue? Roman Holiday? If I marry my friend, I know precisely where it's going. Wife of college president, balancing hospitality duties for faculty and funders on one side with my work at the foundation on the other. I can pretty much plot out my life. But Stern Grove, that was just a lark—a break in the plan, a very welcome interlude between yesterday and tomorrow."

"I think you gave more than you got, Bonnie."

"Oh, Ben, when you and Nick dropped into my life, or we dropped into yours, it was a most precious moment. No agenda. I'll never forget it."

Joyce sighed. "Ben, I can finally tell the truth. It wasn't conniving Joyce who decided to slide into your backside at Stern Grove. It was Bonnie's idea. She has never met a random act of kindness she didn't want to be part of. She saw you looking

repetition

after your brother and that's all it took. She whispered to me, "'I want to meet this guy. Do something.' And so I did."

I led them out to the front porch and we sat down on an old-fashioned swing. I was in the middle. Magnolias, azaleas, irises and ferns bloomed under the Palm Avenue palms.

"There is a season for everything, isn't there?" said Bonnie, staring out at the precisely manicured gardens.

"Ecclesiastes." Joyce and I spoke it together.

I hitched a ride with Joyce to an Audi dealer not far from her place. On the way we talked about music, the revels, and how everything seemed to be back on track with Nick. And then the topic was Bonnie.

"You're pretty observant for a guy," Joyce said as we pulled up in front of the Audi dealer. "She's torn over whether to marry the ex-priest. I am betting she will marry him. She may like larks but deep down she wants an agenda. Growing up in a wealthy family, you know, *noblesse oblige* and all that. She could afford a lark or two now and then. But her life has been based on her religious community's agenda. She's used to it."

"What about you?" I asked.

"What about me?"

"Going with somebody?"

"Are you kidding? Too much in my life right now. And I do scare off some men who are interested. Wealthy realtor, independent, opinionated...oh yeah, and just a little bitter." She laughed at herself.

I smiled, but didn't disagree. As we pulled into the dealership, Joyce said, "Let me know if you need anything. Bonnie's here for a few more days, and I'm around...doing my thing."

I reached over and squeezed her hand. She squeezed back and gave me a brief kiss on the cheek.

I reached for the door handle but then blurted out, "I have a letter."

"A letter?"

"He had mail at the Fairfield Post Office. It's from my wife.

I'll tell you about it after I open it. With Nick. I started to open it, but I stopped."

"Good idea," she said. It didn't take much to imagine what she'd have said if I hadn't.

Within the hour I was behind the wheel of a leased 1997 Audi roadster, hightailing back to San Mateo with the top down. Tomorrow, Big Sur. And the letter from my wife.

Can a person purchase amends? Would a ride in a new Audi amount to admission that my hostility to Nick had been hurtful? I hoped so. Nick thought of himself as Frederick, the field-mouse poet who brightened the winter of life for his family of elders with fanciful stories, summer colors and the sun's rays. I would never know how many lives he had touched, spinning stories of a sun that never set. The car was symbolic. The best amend I could make to Nick was to enjoy the stories.

Early the next morning, I drove the Audi up to Sunnyslope to pick him up. It was mid-September. I had been here for two weeks, but it seemed like a year.

Despite my big mistakes, Consuela had adopted "Nick's brother." I knew how generous that act was, for as far as she was concerned I was an even badder boy than Nick. I was the one who had gotten Nick nearly killed. Me, the prodigal son. Imagine that.

It was eight in the morning and everyone was on the lawn, including Arnie and Rudy, all dressed up in somewhat-next-to-new slacks and shirts. There was whooping and hollering over the Audi. We took time to give rides to all of Sunnyslope—Nick waited until everyone had taken a spin.

"Unbelievably gorgeous," he murmured. He ran his hands across the Audi's sleek hood. "Where do I sign?"

"On to Big Sur!" I smiled.

"Capital, brother. Let's get the hell out of town." He opened the passenger door and fell into the seat. He looked pale. He was breathing hard, and the breaths were shallow. We put on our Giants baseball caps. I honked the horn as we pulled out of Sunnyslope's driveway and headed for Half Moon Bay and Highway 1. I figured we'd take the scenic route down and Highway 101 on the way back.

"Does it get better than this, bro?" he said. He had a kind of Red Baron demeanor, leaning forward into the breeze, holding his flopping cap, locking his eyes on the road.

Nick kept punching buttons in search of the best jazz music as we sped through Pescadero Marsh National Preserve, then on to Santa Cruz, Monterey Bay and Monterey, then past Carmel.

We spent a good deal of the drive talking about Bonnie and Joyce. His breathing seemed labored. I told him about Bonnie and her ex-priest friend. He seemed surprisingly empathetic, no jokes. He did not claim that only he could give her help in making a decision to marry.

We arrived at Pfeiffer Big Sur State Park at one in the afternoon. Our destination further ahead: Nepenthe Restaurant on the ocean side of Highway 1. "Legendary" suited Nepenthe, with its storied beginning in the 1940s and with characters like Rita Hayworth, Orson Welles, Henry Miller. It was a great place to summon ghosts.

When we arrived, the sky was clear and the sun was high. We were able to grab a place for two on the cliffside patio. Like a couple of tourists we both ordered the ambrosia burger, fries and the berry pie with ice cream. Nick observed how the Phoenix Bird sculpture nearby epitomized his own rebirth as lord of the revels. We drank a mineral water toast to Esalen just down the road.

"I'm sorry, brother, for not showing you a better time in old Baghdad by the Bay. Next time. We'll make time for Esalen. We'll visit the monks at the Camaldolese monastery. We'll meditate on life and death here at Land's End."

"Are you afraid of dying, Nick?"

Nick shot me a scorching look. I didn't blame him. It *was* abrupt. He could talk about death in the abstract but not with him in its sights. He gazed intently at the timeless scene of the sky's wraparound horizon and the earth's booming ocean. He gestured with his hands, building a skyscraper level by level, or climbing Devil's Tower inch by inch. "You know the hierarchy of needs by Maslow, yes?"

"Of course. You've burned it into my memory."

"Well, see those waves out there? They're the pyramid. We spend a lifetime climbing the pyramid, like a surfer wriggling up a wave, don't we? We satisfy our physiological needs first, we reach homeostasis, the steadiness of physical health, sex, eating, shitting. Then safety, then love and belonging, then esteem, and then self-actualization." His hands had moved up step by step. "And when we get to the top, like a surfer ready to ride the crest, when we have finally reached creativity and spontaneity, a moral sense, why then what happens?"

He shuddered, let his arms drop and continued in a quieter voice. "The wave collapses and the bottom fucking falls out! Systems shut down! The pyramid collapses under its own weight. After all that work of years, crawling up the wall of identity, inch by inch." His arms flailed on the tabletop, like the flippers of a beached porpoise on the sand.

"We are all just *newcomers* on the tip of Abraham's pyramid—so long to get there, so soon dead. One last big wave, and we hang up the surfing board. That is a profoundly sad moment."

Self, self, self, I thought. "Where do children fit on the pyramid? Did you ever want children?"

"Who wants to know?" asked Nick.

"Just me. Don't they fit on Abraham's ladder? Somewhere between the rung of sex, eating, begetting, and the rung of love? Anywhere, anywhere!"

He seemed to ponder that a moment. "When one's a narcissist, children get in the way. I made the decision about children early on. Remember Avignon? Remember Madeleine?"

Nick and I had made a trip to the south of France many years before, in our twenties, over the Christmas holidays. Nick had just dumped his most recent fiancée.

The trip was fresh in my mind. "Here's what I remember. After many glasses of rum in some cafe, you told me you were ready for love, now that you'd had a vasectomy."

"Dead on, bro."

"You had a newly acquired Bolex camera hoisted on a unipod. You called yourself an *auteur,* said you were creating an art film of your life. We split up halfway through the trip. I went back to Paris and you stayed in Provence, where you met the lovely Madeleine. You told me she relieved you of your Bolex after a hot tryst."

"She was a thief, that lady."

"You said you felt castrated by the theft. A little overboard, I thought, but I was inspired to write a poem about you."

Nick half-rose out of his seat. "You wrote a poem about me, brother? How did it go?"

The France vacation was long before San Francisco, but the trip signaled his full-throated embrace of becoming a character, a larger-than-life solitary figure, the guy for whom humanistic psychology was invented. He had bought his first western-style jacket, complete with fringes, and he wore a broad-brimmed hat day and night. His Bolex recorded his adventures, including images of him with the light-fingered Madeleine. The film was long gone, along with the rest of his possessions.

"Well, it went like this," I said. By now most of the other people on the patio had left. I stood and started gesturing so I could remember the words better. He was all smiles at my overacting.

> *My brother rides there fearlessly*
> *In coat of cowboy thread.*
> *Relentlessly he splits the miles*
> *In quest of freedom's bed.*

"Fearlessly. I *was* fearless," Nick interrupted. "Thank you for the affirmation! What a brother!"

I went on.

> *A Don Quixote for our times,*
> *With Bolex finely honed.*
> *He writes the romance of his life*
> *In Kodak Ektachrome.*

"Right. It wasn't about sex. It was about the romance of life. You know, I was the man of La Mancha."

I went on.

> *A redress of the tilt of time,*
> *A reach for roots in France.*
> *He prods his clacking third-class train,*
> *And charges sans souciance.*

"Capital, brother. *Sans souciance.* Without a care for the present. Reaching for roots. Pushing back time. Oh boy!"

> *So quaff a pint of Guinness now,*
> *And leave your would-be wife.*
> *The well of darkling ego plumb,*
> *The lineaments of life.*

His face flushed with pride. "I *was* a plumber of the psyche! I put aside marriage so I could devote myself to a more humane society for everyone. I became the go-to guy for getting everybody's shit together. You have just distilled the essence of Nick-ness." He stood and gave me a bear hug.

We sat down. My poem had flowed out of a time when, totally unaware, I had started to grieve over the loss of my brother as I knew him. He seemed hallucinatory even then—over forty years ago. That moment marked the beginning of a tear in the fiber of our brotherhood. But it thrilled him now.

I spoke with difficulty. "I never plumbed the well of darkling ego as you set out to do. I was content to hang out on the surface of self-analysis. I envied your free spirit, your thrust against whatever life threw at you. To me *you* were the favored son, the one with gifts that wouldn't stop. Then you went a little crazy. And I went a little controlling. You turned into a drunk and a pothead. Me, an asshole. But I never quit loving you, even when I hated you."

Nick sighed, "I don't recall becoming a drunk or a pothead." He smiled. "As to...." He stopped himself. Yet another surprise.

After we'd finished our pie, I reached into my pocket for the letter. Nick looked puzzled. I opened the envelope and focused again on the familiar stationery that was my wife's. I tried to breathe deeply. "It's a letter to you from Jeanne Marie. It was in the mail we picked up. It's dated just months before she died. You must have filed it away in a closet at Land's End Aloft and forgot about it. It ended up in a dead-letter envelope in Fairfield."

"The mail at the post office?"

"Yes." I gulped for air. I felt lightheaded, my stomach was stirring "I haven't read it."

"Read it."

And I did.

> *Dear Nick,*
>
> *This will be my last letter to you for a while. I'm asking you a favor. Please, please, never tell Ben anything about what I've shared with you as one addict to another. Ben knows my story, of course. He's had to live with me. But he doesn't know the whole story. The crazy things I've done to keep supplied. You know what I mean. How many lies I've told him to avoid making him suspicious, to keep the pills coming. How close I was to the edge. You and I both know he really doesn't want to know the whole story, but that isn't for me to deal with now.*
>
> *This is my big year. I'm turning a corner. I've been clean for a month. I get the feeling from Ben that he wants*

to talk to you. If he does, please don't tell him anything I've shared with you here or in the past. Leave that to me. I'll tell him in my own good time.

Meanwhile, thank you for everything you've done for me. The imaging exercises, the affirmations, the whole therapy-by-phone thing.

I stopped reading and looked at him. I thought I knew what the next sentence was going to be. Did he? He laid his arms on the table and put his head down, hiding his face. Not a good sign.

Most of all, I thank you <u>for refusing to supply me with pills</u>. I was so angry that you wouldn't help me. And the time you gave me a batch of sugar pills—you bastard! But now I'm so much stronger, I'm grateful.

I reread the paragraph. She had underlined those words as if she wanted to make sure I would know some day.

I started reading again.

I know you've got your own problems. Big ones. You can do me—us—another favor by really getting help for yourself. Ben has lost faith in you, I know. It's hard for him to understand how deep despair and isolation are for some of us. I know that deep down he loves you. I fear for you, brother-in-law. And remember: a day at a time.

With love, Jeanne Marie

At that moment I missed Jeanne Marie more than I had in a long time. I could hear her voice, her healthy self. In that letter she was reaching out to a fellow addict, and trying to shield me at the same time.

Nick raised his head and gazed out to sea. "Are you surprised?" he asked.

"Yes. And relieved."

"Not as much as I am."

I believed him. He had no recall of how he had answered her plea for pills. But something in him back then had said no.

We sat there another half-hour or so, just looking at the ocean, the breakers, the cliffs, the seagulls. Music flowed from somewhere in the building. Pachelbel's Canon. Nick conducted the music with his index finger. Every once in a while, I hummed the melody.

On the way home we took the quicker route via Highway 101. He asked me to stop in a little town just off the highway. He said he knew a small store that sold sparklers. We stopped and bought several packages.

Promptly at six-thirty we arrived back at Sunnyslope. José was outside waiting for us. Arnie and Rudy were sitting in the metal patio chairs sending up their smoky contribution to pollution.

José approached. "Hey, Ben, Happy Birthday!"

I had totally forgotten today was my birthday. And I realized Nick had spread the word.

"Happy Birthday, brother," he said, smiling as if really pleased with himself. I helped him out of the car and gave him a hug.

José took my hand and led me toward the door. Arnie and Rudy stood like an honor guard at a parade. Both men waved cigarettes as we walked into the house. Inside, Joyce and Bonnie were arranging steaming bowls of food on the table. Frieda and Consuela were bringing more plates from the kitchen. Barney was seated at one of the folding chairs that had been added to the dining room table. Nick and I had just a few seconds to hug Joyce and Bonnie before Consuela clapped her hands together.

She snapped off the TV and started a prayer in Spanish, which Arnie and Rudy sat through stoically. Frieda lit two candles on the table and whacked Arnie's arm with a fork when he tried to light a cigarette off one of them. Everybody laughed.

Consuela held up a glass of apple cider. "Now, Ben, we are very happy to have your surprise party here." In Spanish and English she told everyone to eat, several times.

Beans, rice and pork tostadas—I'd never tasted Mexican food as good. Joyce badgered Frieda for the recipes. She and Bonnie kept looking across the table at Nick and me, checking for any signals about the success or failure of our Big Sur afternoon. After dinner Frieda emerged from the kitchen with a huge chocolate cake decorated with one row of six red candles and one row of three green ones. They sang to me, I blew out the candles, and Frieda ladled out generous cuts of cake.

Now I knew why Nick had requested the sparkler stop. He stood up and gave a little speech. "Actually, my brother is older than me, not younger, but what are a few years, more or less, among brothers?" He looked over at me. "Okay, I lied. Anyway, we've missed saying 'Happy Birthday' to each other the last many years. I'm happy to be here for this one, bro. Happy Birthday!"

Then Bonnie stood. "Thank you, Consuela, for inviting us to Ben's party. I have to leave the country for a few weeks tomorrow. I am so glad I was here." She looked at me. "In grade school we always had the children write a few sentences on the highlights of their summer. Well, this summer, I met Ben and Nick." She leaned over and kissed my brother and me.

Joyce stood and sang a few lines of the Cole Porter lyrics about the many ways somebody beloved was the tops. She blew Nick and me a kiss and ended on "You're the tops!"

"Speech, speech," Barney yelled at me, the first words out of his mouth—ever?

"I just want to say...." What was it I wanted to say? "Nick and I drove to Big Sur country today. I totally forgot it was my birthday. That's life with Nick. I'm glad I finally took the time to reconnect with you, brother. I've had to throw away my agenda these last two weeks. I never would have met all these people if not for you. Thank you, all."

Nick held up a package of sparklers. No time for dead air in this crowd. "Let's go light up the night." He took Frieda's hand and started a little samba line out the front door. Even Barney joined in, accompanied by Bonnie and Joyce on either side. José lit the sparklers one by one, and we stood in a circle, waving the sticks. There were shrieks of delight from Consuela and Frieda. Rudy and Arnie were grinning quietly. Barney kept his sparkler at arm's length, just staring at it.

Pretty soon some neighbor families came across their lawns. The circle kept getting larger as children and parents joined in. People swayed back and forth, and José was kept busy replacing spent sparklers with new ones. When the last sparkler was just a tiny, glowing tip of red, the circle broke. Neighbors stayed to chat with the men of Sunnyslope and wish me a happy birthday. I met at least three parents whose kids spoke familiarly of Grandpa Nick, Grandpa Arnie, Grandpa Rudy and Grandpa Barney. Cunning old Nick had achieved grandparent status despite his vasectomy.

Bonnie and Joyce, Nick and I stood in the driveway, saying our goodbyes. Arnie and Rudy watched from the porch. Smoking, of course. I wanted to talk to the women about the Big Sur adventure, but it would wait. For Bonnie, it would wait a little longer.

"Goodnight, you guys. And goodbye for now," said Bonnie. Her flight to Quito left early in the morning.

Nick grilled her—how would the nighttime revels grant ever be secured now that she was off "slumming in some grimy, rat-infested shanty town in some jungle in South America?" Bonnie assured him she would be in touch with her Uncle Matthew and would stay on top of the funding process.

"We're talking real money here, Bonnie! I'm invested!" he confided to her. She and Joyce beamed—I think they were as happy as I was about his proprietary interest in guiding the growth of the Night Revels program.

Bonnie hugged me. "Goodbye, Ben. For now. I have a feeling we'll see each other again."

"Hey, what secrets are you telling him that you're not telling me?" yelled Nick.

"Nothing, just where I keep the keys to my apartment!" said Bonnie. She took his arm as we walked to their car and nuzzled his ear with her nose. Joyce and I slid our arms around each other's backs and followed. I was considering kissing her cheek just as she turned to me and brushed her lips across mine.

"Goodnight, ladies." Nick blessed them with arm outstretched. "Honk if you love Jesus." Joyce honked and they drove off. Nick and I walked back, past the Audi to the porch where the lads were having one last smoke.

"Thanks for arranging the party, Nick. It was a great surprise."

"Funny the stuff I didn't forget." This time he hugged me.

In the rearview mirror, I watched him watch me drive away until the night and the fog obscured him. Misfortune had finally melted my heart.

"Ben! Ben! They just took Nick to the hospital!" It was José, shouting into the telephone at the B&B. I looked at the clock. It was seven in the morning. José said Nick had cried out and when José went to his room he found him not breathing. José gave him CPR until the paramedics arrived. The hospital was in San Mateo. Nick was not doing well. I fumbled with my pants and shirt, threw on a jacket and followed José's directions to the hospital.

Nick was on oxygen and breathing with the help of a ventilator. His eyes were closed. I thought of my first sight of him a few weeks ago, in front of Sunnyslope. He had looked like a cartoon character, waiting to be sprung from a nursing home.

Minutes later, Consuela and Frieda solemnly entered the hospital room. They were clutching rosaries. This solidarity almost made me weep. Into the anonymous high-tech world of end-of-life maintenance, they and their beads proclaimed something beautiful. Something nostalgic. Something essentially human. Consuela kissed Nick's face, and cried. Frieda squeezed his shoulders, massaging them like dough with her strong fingers. Talk about family. Talk about hands-on mourning.

Nick stopped breathing at about ten that morning. Nurses and a medic were fluttering around the room. I remembered the discussion about "Do not resuscitate" at Saint Francis Memorial. One of the nurses showed me a form. "Brother recommends against resuscitation." I nodded.

I called Joyce and left a message. I suspected she was dropping Bonnie at the airport. I signed papers for the hospital, and an hour later, someone from the county morgue showed up and had me sign more. And then a mortician came in, talked to us in quiet tones and with the help of a nurse lifted Nick's body onto a gurney. Consuela, Frieda and I held each other and gave a final goodbye wave.

I followed the women back to Sunnyslope in the Audi. As we drove up, I saw a couple of young mothers leading their kids outside onto their front lawns. Word of his death had spread. The kids picked up spent sparklers from last night and started waving the forlorn sticks in the morning sun.

Joyce was at Sunnyslope when we got there. After a while, she asked me to follow her back to her place. We both knew what was going to happen. Alone in the Audi, I smiled at what Nick would have to say about it. "About time," for starters. Maybe even a hallelujah.

She was a quiet, intense lover. My body was no prize, but it didn't seem to matter.

Lying in bed the next morning, I read Joyce the letter. She took it from me and reread it silently. She cried when she finished it and held me for a long time.

It was late afternoon when Joyce finally checked her phone messages. One was from Bonnie. Joyce put it on speaker. "Joyce, I just arrived at the hotel. A bumpy ride. Please, call me today. How's Nick? How's Ben doing? I send love to you all. *Call me.*"

Joyce called her and told her Nick had died. She passed the phone to me. It was strange, talking to Bonnie on the phone and lying on Joyce's bed. I got up and walked with the phone to my ear.

Bonnie asked me to talk about Big Sur. I told her everything. There was a long silence when I finished. She sniffled a few times. "Oh, Ben," she whispered. "I've dreamed about Nick, banishing sundown, believing in nothing, but somehow believing in everything. Except doubt. And now you know how he loved you and your wife."

"You're right. I'm glad he lived long enough for me to know."

When I said goodbye, I could tell she knew I hadn't spent the night on the sofa bed or the spare room.

I spent an hour later that day on the phone with my daughters. I had kept Nick at a distance from them, too. I knew they had wanted to keep a connection with him, no matter what I needed, but I'd discouraged them, sometimes straight out, sometimes subtly—or so I thought. I owed them an apology. "You would have liked him," I said, and knew it was the most honest confession I could make.

I made arrangements for Nick's cremation. I placed a small death notice in the *Chronicle*. "Therapist. Formerly on staff of California Veterans Health Services. Proud Member of Elder Town community. Survived by brother Ben and nieces Clare and Frances. Deepest thanks to Andrea, program director. Many thanks to the Sunnyslope Board and Care Residence, to Consuela, José and Frieda. Donations to Elder Town, please."

The paperwork proved to be a couple of days' work. There were more forms from the state and the county, forms for release of his assets, which were not enough to cover the cremation fees, much less the urn.

Joyce had work to do, so I spent the days handling the minutiae of death or hanging out at Sunnyslope. Nights were at Joyce's.

Three days later I received the call that I could pick up the ashes and the urn from the mortician. I called Andrea. She asked me to come over. She led me to her office and told me the guests at Elder Town had requested that there be no service.

"When one of them dies, the book is closed," she said. "Even for Nick. Death is always on their minds. I've had some unfortunate episodes when we did hold services. I'm so sorry, Ben." I said I understood and that Nick would probably be the first to say amen. He'd want to be remembered as a living, breathing spark of wit and wickedness.

On the way out, she showed me a blown-up photograph of Nick plucking Excalibur at the revels. It had been taped to the wall outside the activity room. Someone had scrawled in pencil at the bottom of the picture. "To our Nicky. You are going to the sun." Everyone had signed it.

So did I.

That evening, Joyce and I drove to the Great Highway near Noriega Street—at sunset. She brought a picnic basket, and I brought the urn. We stopped at Nick's Great Highway address and she placed a sprig of fresh flowers near the sidewalk. We went across the highway, climbed up the path to the top of the dune, and scrambled down onto Ocean Beach.

The sun illuminated the sand and the water with blinding translucence. It was getting cold, and out of nowhere the fog rolled in. I opened the urn, took a handful of ashes and heaved them into the wind. I held the urn for Joyce. She used both hands and flung the ashes high. We watched as the wind played with them.

"The rest goes back to North Dakota," I said. "He once said he wanted his ashes both at Land's End and in Bismarck."

"Funny, he still thought of North Dakota as home."

"I think he wanted to be close so he could haunt me from St. Mary's Cemetery. That is, if I can get the priest to bury him there." I tossed more ashes into the breeze.

Joyce uncorked a bottle of California wine and spread a tablecloth next to the urn. We ate Manchego cheese on crackers and forkfuls of chicken salad. She produced a bottle of non-alcoholic beer, took a pull and passed it to me. Then she emptied the rest on the sand and said, "Here's to you, Nick. We watched the beer drain slowly, slowly into Ocean Beach.

As the sun disappeared, we packed up the picnic basket, climbed to the top of the dune and then across the Great Highway to the Audi.

"Let's go to Stern Grove!" I said on impulse. "Reenact the scene of the crime."

"I love it," answered Joyce.

We drove, parked at 19th and Sloat, and strode down to the esplanade. Stern Grove was closed to the public. A security guard waved us over. "We just want to sit in the meadow for ten minutes," Joyce cajoled him. "Remembering a friend who just died." The guard, a burly fellow whose face bristled with authority growled something about "rules are rules," but he let us in.

We found a place at the bottom of the hill. She sat behind me. "On three," I said, and counted. "One, two, three."

Joyce slid down the soft, dewy grass, legs apart until she was wrapped around my hips. She encircled my midsection with her arms and held me tight. After a minute, she leaned back, pulling my head on top of her stomach, and we gazed up at what we could see of the night sky.

"Want to know why I really agreed to slide into you?" She sat up and bent over me.

"Yes I do."

"It was the program."

"The program?"

"Any guy in his sixties who plunks down an eight-and-a-half-by-eleven-inch glossy program on damp ground and then settles down on top of it, knowing he's going to look awfully silly when he stands and reveals a dry bull's eye on the wet bottom of his slacks, well...."

She was laughing so hard now she could hardly get the rest out. "That man does not stand on ceremony. He has no guile. That guy...is not sour. I thought I would like to know a man like that."

"All right, that's it." It was the security guard, a flashlight in his hand searching us out. Joyce pushed me up and we stood and brushed each other off. The beam hit us squarely in the face, and we felt our way across the meadow.

We trudged over to where he stood. "Thanks," I said. He just nodded and grunted, pointing to the road. Joyce and I breathed hard as we pushed our way up the steep grade. Pretty soon the streetlights at 19th and Sloat were visible. She stopped climbing and squeezed my arm.

"When you go back to North Dakota, you're going to leave one unhappy woman here."

I felt myself slip back toward my past, a cautious lover, a rational man. "You'll be busy selling high-priced real estate. I'll be busy teaching Latin."

"What kind of excuse is that? You need another kick in your damp butt!"

I blurted out Nick's observation: "A fallen woman."

"If he only knew how hard I'd fallen." We laughed hard as we climbed the last few yards to Sloat Boulevard.

As we slid into the car, she reached across and whispered, "About me being happy just selling real estate and you teaching Latin, Nick would call that kind of talk 'noise' and you know what he thought should be done to noise."

We started the drive to Geary and Gough streets. Joyce was softly massaging the back of my neck. "So tell me," she said, "about this Aeneas guy that you and Bonnie obsessed over. The one who ditched his girlfriend and talked about people shedding tears over the suffering of others."

"Long story. An epic, actually."

"I've got time."

That was the truth of it. We both had time. All we had to do was take it.

Acknowledgments

The manuscript for this book was languishing on my laptop in 2012 when I met Ann Ryan. Her steady, professional guidance as editor cut away most of the chaff and immeasurably enriched the wheat of the story. Every writer *needs* an editor and I'm grateful she agreed to be mine.

Thanks to Susan McKenna and Bridget Murphy for their critical reading of various versions of the manuscript. Thanks also to Virginia Randolph Bueide for many encouraging words. Finally, thank you to my wife Ruth Murphy, who has supported my writing, as the Irish would say: through "tick and tin."